Time Flight

Time Flight

SUSAN SYERS STARK

LeafStormPress

SANTA FE, NEW MEXICO

LEAF STORM PRESS
Post Office Box 4670
Santa Fe, NM 87502
LeafStormPress.com

Leaf Storm logo is a trademark of Leaf Storm Press LLC.

For information about special discounts for bulk purchases,
please email LeafStormPress@gmail.com.

PUBLISHER's NOTE:
This book is a work of fiction. Names, characters, places, and incidents
are either a product of the author's imagination or used fictitiously.

ISBN 978-0-9914105-5-2

Library of Congress Control Number: 2014946475

First Edition

Printed in the United States of America

Publisher's Cataloging-in-Publication Data

(Provided by Quality Books, Inc.)
Stark, Susan Syers.
Time flight / Susan Syers Stark. -- First edition.
pages cm
SUMMARY: A young boy's curiosity leads him through a
magical portal into a land of fantasy and imagination
where he meets a series of eccentric characters.
Audience: 8-12.
LCCN 2014946475
ISBN 978-0-9914105-5-2

1. Voyages, Imaginary--Juvenile fiction. 2. Time
travel--Juvenile fiction. 3. Fantasy fiction.
[1. Voyages, Imaginary--Fiction. 2. Time travel--Fiction.
3. Fantasy.] I. Title.

PZ7.S79455Tim 2014   [Fic]
QBI14-600155

To Richard, my best listener

Contents

A Beginning

Anthony would always say the Adventure began that moment he saw Mr. Trippett's necktie—that sky blue necktie with the golden kite sailing off into the puffy clouds, though tethered securely to Mr. Trippett's neck.

"Yes, that's when it all began," Anthony would say, closing his eyes to see clearly to that deep place of memory. "That kite necktie led me right to the Boulders."

But who knows precisely when any Adventure really begins. Certainly this is Anthony's story, so we could start with the necktie. Perhaps, however, this story began thousands, even millions, of years ago when that very patch of ground known now as "The Park" to Centerville citizens experienced massive subterranean shifting, quakings and spewings, coughings and hissings, and an icy deposit of granite boulders of immense size. Just perhaps this Adventure of Anthony Bartholomew Mandopolis began then.

Or, just maybe it started with the note...

CHAPTER 1

The Note

It was the end of another school day in Mrs. Quickett's third-grade classroom at Willow Elementary School. The children were noisy, collecting lunch kits and jackets, packing up backpacks and oozing that giddy excitement that sometimes comes with a March afternoon quite full of wind. For exactly two minutes they were allowed to ready themselves for dismissal. Mrs. Quickett was timing them. But she, too, sensed an unusual jingly-jangly sort of energy in the classroom.

Barometric pressure, she thought to herself, while scanning the room to find Anthony Mandopolis at the fish tank again. Mrs. Quickett was a master at multitasking.

"Just making the most of my time," she said quietly as she straightened a stack of spelling tests on the corner of her desk, helped Annabelle with her jacket, and fed the class guinea pig a bite of apple left from lunch, all the while checking on Anthony. "Anthony," she said, pausing a half-second. "Anthony," she repeated a bit louder. Generally Anthony required two signals.

"Oh, sorry, Mrs. Quickett." Anthony's face rose above the aquarium. "Here I am, just looking for the angelfish. I think he's hiding in the castle." Anthony smiled all the way to her desk, wondering how it would be to spend the night in an underwater castle with an angelfish.

Mrs. Quickett handed Anthony a typed letter, unfolded and stapled to yesterday's math paper.

"Please give this to your parents," she said gently. "And let's work harder tomorrow to make better use of our time."

Mrs. Quickett always used *we* and *us* in ways that seemed strange to Anthony. After all, she did use her time well. She was, in fact, a Timer. She wore no jewelry except that big-faced wristwatch which she referred to constantly. She used all three timers on her desk to keep her classroom "moving along." She cautioned her students about wasting time, even killing time—a phrase which generally sent Anthony into an imaginative place where an ancient, bearded man lay in a heap upon the damp stone floor of a dungeon with only talking rats for company.

Mrs. Quickett often quoted Benjamin Franklin. "Lost time is never found again!" And Anthony wondered where one might search for lost time... if one had the time to do such a thing.

Mrs. Quickett timed everything down to the second. She timed math tests, Free Reading, restroom breaks, and lining up for lunch. One time she even timed the class as they wrote poems. Their poems were about clocks. And although Mrs. Quickett was a gentle person and Anthony felt she liked him, she lately appeared weary, mostly with him.

"We have one minute before the bell rings, Anthony. Enough time for me to read this note to you. I want you to understand the importance of how you use your time, Anthony. I want your parents to understand this problem we are having."

Anthony's round brown eyes widened.

"Thank you, Mrs. Quickett," he said, eager to hear her comments about his math page and especially problem #9. In #9 Mrs. Quickett was the main character. She was selling minutes. That was her job, a minute salesclerk. Anthony loved that problem best. He had even illustrated it. He wondered how she liked his drawing.

"Dear Mr. and Mrs. Mandopolis," Mrs. Quickett read. "I am very concerned with Anthony's use of time in our classroom. He cannot seem to stay on track. He daydreams. He drifts. He forgets his assignments and rarely finishes his classwork on time.

Anthony is such a wonderful boy! He is our model for loving-kindness and we all love his stories!" Here Mrs. Quickett stopped and smiled briefly at Anthony. "However, he simply MUST learn to use his time more productively. Attached is yesterday's math page. You will see that it is unfinished. When I spoke with Anthony about it, he told me he had just finished it "another way." I welcome your suggestions. Please sign and return ASAP. Yours truly, Willa Quickett."

"Thank you, Mrs. Quickett," Anthony sighed, wondering if she had even seen the picture he had drawn of her selling minutes. He had beamed at her mention of his stories, but then he tried to find his serious face. There was nothing new in this note home. He knew he was a dreamer, but was that bad? He simply couldn't seem to keep from imagining stories.

His parents knew all of this, too, for Anthony was gifted by generations of storytellers in his family. Anthony's father was a storyteller, and his father and grandfather before him. Once his Uncle Alfred rode a bus from Jackson, Tennessee, to Big Spring, Texas, gathering stories from every single passenger and writing them down in a faded blue notebook. Uncle Alfred gave that notebook to Anthony. It was right under his bed with other treasures.

"You have inherited an amazing imagination," his parents would say and smile at their son.

So it is not surprising that taking the note home did not trouble Anthony at all. Most certainly he did not want to be a bother for Mrs. Quickett, but he was happy that something he had created on his math page had caught her eye. True, the last four problems were not exactly finished, not in the way she had instructed. But Anthony had transformed them. The problems had become stories!

CHAPTER 2

The Necktie

Anthony left school that day looking at the sky. The March afternoon had turned cloudy, and large grey thunderheads tumbled about overhead. He was so busy watching a huge elephant-shaped cloud merge with a sort of dragon-lizard that he almost forgot to stop at the crosswalk and wait for Mr. Trippett, the crossing guard.

Mr. Trippett was a special friend to all of Willow's students. He had been safely guiding children across Elm Street for years. He knew all their names and whether they liked baseball or soccer or reading or art. He even knew the names of their dogs.

Anthony always looked forward to crossing Elm Street because Mr. Trippett never hurried. He walked slowly. He spoke slowly. He always had time to visit.

After so much hurrying at school, Anthony felt like his time with Mr. Trippett was like taking a long, deep breath.

Mr. Trippett had huge, bushy eyebrows and a nose so large it seemed to be attached to his glasses. Anthony studied him secretly. He knew it was impolite to stare, but he wondered if a nose like that could be real. Perhaps Mr. Trippett was a circus clown disguised as a crossing guard with his funny eyebrows, his attached nose, his big rubber boots, and a different necktie every day. Even if it was snowing, Mr. Trippett had on a necktie, if necessary wearing it over his heavy jacket.

"It's Mr. Trippett's trademark," Anthony's mother had said one day. "He wants you children to look around and see things... the necktie is just his reminder."

Anthony needed no encouragement to look at Mr. Trippett's necktie each afternoon. That necktie was like a story in chapters. Each day he made up a new necktie story, related, of course, to the story from the day before. Yesterday Mr. Trippett had worn a polar-bear necktie. Today it was a kite, a golden kite sailing about in a beautiful blue sky.

As Mr. Trippett neared, Anthony told himself a short story of a polar bear that accidentally released the kite and asked all his animal friends to help him capture it. So far only the ostrich and the orangutan had agreed. The zebra was too busy with appointments.

Very often Mr. Trippett and Anthony played a word game when they walked together across Elm Street. In their conversations Mr. Trippett would use what he called a five-dollar word, a word probably new to Anthony. Anthony tried to guess it, and its meaning. If he got both answers right, he would earn five dollars of imaginary money. So far Anthony had eighty-five dollars in his word account with Mr. Trippett and seventeen words from this game alone in his red spiral notebook, his very own dictionary. For Anthony collected words, like his mother collected watering cans. His red spiral dictionary held this collection.

"Great wind today, Anthony," said Mr. Trippett as Anthony approached the curb. "Fine day for a kite." He paused. "Do you have a kite, Anthony? Or something to fly in this *boisterous* wind?"

"No, sir," said Anthony, watching the wiry arms of the elm trees waving about. "No, kite," he said quietly to himself, thinking about that word boisterous.

"Well, that's likely a good thing, young fella. A very good thing. Today a kite might just lift a little fella like you right off the ground and carry you far away to a place where you couldn't even speak the language. Yep. That's surely what might happen if you were to go and fly a kite this particular day. I think you're plumb lucky not to have a kite at all. We'd likely never see hide nor hair of you again.

On the other hand," Mr. Trippett's bushy eyebrows arched into small mountains above his dancing eyes. He held out his other hand and Anthony shook it in their usual joking way. "On the other hand," he repeated, "a kite just might fly you to the moon and back. You never know what might happen with the wind and a kite, Anthony." Mr. Trippett squinted his eyes and nodded his head at such a possibility.

Anthony's large, brown eyes had shifted from the trees to a distant place in the sky. He was imagining the swirl, the gust, the energy of a wind strong enough to lift all sixty-three pounds of him twirling and spinning like a puff of cloud into a place far from Elm Street, where he stood with Mr. Trippett.

Mr. Trippett recognized that look. "Anthony," he said. "Anthony," he repeated, raising his voice over the sound of a school bus pulling out of the parking lot.

Now Mr. Trippett was bending down, very close to Anthony. Close enough for Anthony to really inspect his large nose, crisscrossed like a roadmap with red highways. But Anthony chose not to look at the nose. He chose instead to look at the golden kite necktie.

Mr. Trippett was close enough to see Anthony's eyes suddenly blink, shift, and refocus. He was close enough to recognize the look of a plan brewing in the imagination of Anthony Mandopolis.

"See you tomorrow, Mr. Trippett," Anthony said, suddenly turning around and heading down the sidewalk bordering Elm Street. "Boisterous, Mr. Trippett! Boisterous! That's the word! I think it means...maybe loud?" Anthony had turned now and waited for Mr. Trippett to answer.

"You're right! Another five dollars to your account, Anthony. But aren't you going the wrong way?" Mr. Trippett's eyebrows formed mountains again. He knew Anthony's house was in the opposite direction.

"Oh no, sir. I'm just going to the park. I need to check on this boisterous wind...just a little *sidetrack*."

"Well, then. Pay attention, young fella."

Anthony waved, then turned, smiling to himself. Mr. Trippett always said those exact words. "Pay attention."

CHAPTER 3

The Boulders

The town of Centerville lay in the middle of a great flatness. Wheat fields and cornfields patchworked the land around it. A gentle, slow-moving river twisted its way from mountains fifty miles north, flowed through town, and connected fifty miles south with a larger river. On any map, Centerville looked like the middle bead on a blue ribbon. But middleness was just the reason for the town's name. It was not what made Centerville even mildly famous.

Centerville's moderate fame came from the Boulders, a huge mound of granite rocks, some the size of elephants, which lay heaped in the far corner of Centerville Park. More than just the immensity of the rocks, it was their unexpected location which made them a landmark, for the land around Centerville was deep soiled and rockless.

Some years ago a young, bearded professor from the state college had spent several weeks studying the Boulders, measuring all sorts of things like height and width, temperature and composition. He had made phone calls and charts, stored data, and collected soil—and finally proclaimed that the rocks were *erratics*, a scientific name for boulders that have turned up in an unlikely place. His report, printed in the local paper, stated that evidence suggested that these large rocks were "perhaps the deposits of an ice-age glacier."

The folks of Centerville smiled good-naturedly and said to one another, "Well, what do you know about that! Imagine! A glacier stopping right here in Centerville!"

To all the local citizens, the Boulders were a gigantic playscape of geology and history and just a little bit of local fame. But to Anthony they were like family. He and his father had been climbing these rocks since he was three, and he knew them by heart—the camel rock, the beetle rock, the elephant rock, and, at the very top, the Nest, a rocky hollow formed by the coming together of the topmost boulders. He knew all the trails to the top, the best toeholds and handholds, and where there were ledges just right for resting. He had scooted and balanced and hid and imagined on these rocks. When he stood in that topmost perch and was indeed the tallest thing around, Anthony felt a kinship with the birds. He always felt if the wind were ever strong enough, he might soar all the way across the park, maybe even to Far Away.

That's why, on this windy March afternoon, Anthony was hurrying toward the Boulders in Centerville Park. It was a sidetrack he would never forget.

CHAPTER 4

Leonardo and Icarus

It took Anthony little time to reach the Nest of the Boulders. He knew the shortest way up, and he was filled with the excitement of a bold adventure. When he did reach that rocky hollow, he knew that Mr. Trippett had been right about the wind.

It had a boiling energy, pushing at Anthony from all directions. Standing up within the Nest, he felt the force of a wind that whipped and whirled and swooped and roared. If ever there were a day in which the wind might sweep him out to Far Away, this was it. A boisterous wind!

"Was this the kind of wind Leonardo felt when he dreamed of flight?" Anthony often wondered about Leonardo da Vinci and his sketch of those huge, bat-skeleton wings, awkward and heavy, and pictured in Anthony's *Great Inventions* book. The great da Vinci never tried out those wings, according to the story.

"Maybe he was just too busy thinking up other ideas," Anthony had reasoned. "Maybe he was scolded for wasting time. Maybe he knew the earlier story of Icarus and had decided to attach his dreams of flight to paper only."

"Icarus . . . Icarus . . ." Anthony spoke into the wind.

He loved even the sound of his name. Icarus, who flew with wings of feathers and wax until he foolishly ventured too near the sun and landed in the ocean below. It was a story of daring and foolishness, Anthony's father had told him.

"And not obeying his father," he had said, smiling at Anthony.

Maybe this wind that whipped around him right now was the very same sort of wind that carried Icarus.

Anthony was transported now. His eyes had that faraway look, and his green jacket had become the white tunic of a Greek youth. He was listening yet again to the advice of his imagined father, Daedalus the master craftsman, as he strapped the feathered wings onto his son's shoulders.

"Stay away from the sun, my child, for the wax will most certainly melt," Daedalus warned

Anthony pulled his jacket hood over his head and tied it securely under his chin. Very cautiously, because one lesson of the Icarus story was to be careful, Anthony climbed atop the slanting limestone ledge, which rose to form the very highest flat surface on that whole heap of boulders. Very slowly he stood up, bracing his legs and all sixty-three pounds of him against the wind. The wind roared and whistled around him, but carefully he unzipped his jacket, grabbed its lower edges, and, holding his arms down and straight, imagined himself kite-shaped.

He was prepared to be launched. He waited.

The wind battered Anthony. It circled him, tunneled through his legs, and puffed out his jacket. It howled one moment and whispered the next. Yet Anthony stood firm and ready for lift-off.

And as Waiting Time never hurries, it seemed to Anthony that he stood forever in that hopeful position. The giant swoop he had imagined did not come. Nothing blew him off that slanted perch and sailed him to Far Away.

Finally, reluctantly, Anthony inched his way off the slim ledge and back into the rocky protection of the Nest. He could still feel and hear the wind thrashing and whistling above him.

Oh! How he wished for something to fly!

He thought about his backpack, left at the base of the Boulders when he climbed up. It was filled with paper. He could make dozens of paper airplanes. He glanced over the side of the Nest, considering that climb, all the way down and all the way up again. It was a long way, but he had time—and flying a paper airplane would be almost like flying a kite.

Just as he was heaving himself over the rim of top rocks to the path below, something rustled in his jeans pocket. It was the note from Mrs. Quickett attached to his math-stories page. Right there in his back pocket! Two sheets of paper!

Two paper airplanes!

CHAPTER 5

Launch

Mrs. Quickett's note folded easily—mountain folds, valley folds. Anthony could make a paper airplane with his eyes closed.

Standing up once again within the waist-high protection of the rocky nest, Anthony positioned himself: left arm straight forward and pointing toward the direction of flight, right arm back, fingers firmly holding the belly of the craft, and eyes on that invisible space above and beyond where this plane would sail upward and away.

He waited for that opening within the wind...for the pause, the stillness. If he just looked closely enough, maybe he could even see that opening, like a doorway, where his airplane would enter the currents of the sky.

Waiting...waiting...

There it was! *Swoosh!* Anthony threw the airplane! Up, up, up it soared, riding a magical wave of wind. It sailed exactly as he had hoped. Angling now, pivoting slightly, hesitating, now lifting again, now dipping.

And, as if attached by invisible threads, Anthony's small body moved in duplicate, mirroring the flight of the aircraft. Turning, lifting, soaring. Anthony felt he was flying, too. Flying...flying!

But, just when it seemed the plane had really caught an updraft, it slowed, hovered for a second, and then turned its nose downward in a spiraling fall.

Anthony watched it disappear beyond the far side of the Boulders. He continued to watch the empty space, now filled with sky and the backdrop of trees. The wind had stopped.

Anthony sat down in the Nest, sighed a big sigh and wondered about making a second airplane. He still had his math-stories page. He could use that. But he needed to find Mrs. Quickett's note. That was important. That was being *responsible*.

Just yesterday his dad had talked to him about being responsible, about taking out the garbage and feeding his cat, Selma, and turning in his spelling homework. All of this without being reminded.

"A responsible person doesn't have to be told again and again to do what is expected, what is right," his dad had said in his serious voice.

Anthony knew what was expected here. He zipped up his jacket and heaved himself over the rim of the Nest. He would find his airplane and go home. He would show his parents his math stories and Mrs. Quickett's note. He would be responsible.

And though he didn't know it, his adventure had begun.

CHAPTER 6

A Way

The boulders below him were huge. They huddled together like a gathering of giants and offered no easy passage, especially for a climber with short legs.

But Anthony had read enough stories to know there is always a way through or around or over any sort of obstacle, if one was determined and courageous and used his wits. He was certain that the airplane had lodged somewhere below him and that he would find it. With that sense of *optimism*, a word he had recently entered into his dictionary, he turned over on his stomach and began lowering himself to the rock below.

In that very moment of high hopes, with his whole body clinging to the bald face of rock, Anthony heard something—a deep, far-off rumbling.

When Anthony's toes reached the lower boulder, he crouched down into a small ball. He untied the strings of his jacket hood.

What was that? he wondered.

It wasn't the wind. The wind had stopped. Everything seemed strangely quiet and still.

There it was again! Another deep rumble, long and rolling. It seemed to gather strength, like thunder in an approaching storm. It seemed to be coming from the rocks. Anthony felt the sound.

He sat very still, listening. Again the sound stopped.

Anthony puzzled. He stood up and peered over the side. He scanned the park below, searching for something that could explain these rumbly noises within the Boulders. The park was empty, and there was no sign of the airplane.

Could it be an earthquake? There was no tumbling of these rocks, and even after all that wind, the trees in the park stood strangely still.

Maybe it was the heavy equipment out on Highway 6. Maybe it was construction noise.

Anthony gazed in the direction of Highway 6. For weeks he had been watching those heavy dump trucks and rollers. They were working close to The Burger Barn.

The Burger Barn. Anthony's stomach growled and, swift as thought, he imagined twirling in circles on one of the red vinyl bar stools and waiting for his usual order. He could see it clearly: a large chocolate milkshake with whipped cream oozing down the glass, a Junior Burger, cut the lettuce and onions, and a basket of crispy fries with three little paper cups of ketchup, all on his own brown plastic tray.

Oh my! Anthony was so hungry. He had to get home. Dinner would be ready. His mother might have fixed spaghetti with tiny meatballs and the garlic breadsticks he loved. Or maybe they would all go to Burger Barn.

But first he had to find Mrs. Quickett's note. After dinner he'd tell his parents about this wind and the strange sounds he had heard. He'd tell them how he'd almost taken flight, like Icarus. Then he would give them the note.

Cautiously he scooted down and around the next several boulders. Still there was no path, and Anthony had to press his small body against the rocks, holding to whatever knob or protrusion he could find. And then... the sound again! A deep, heavy jarring sound. Something was shifting in the rocks. He knew it. This was not a sound caused by highway equipment. Something was happening inside this pile of boulders. It was like the boulders were rearranging themselves. Anthony's whole body felt the vibrations.

"Pay attention." Mr. Trippett's words looped through his thoughts.

Anthony looked carefully at the rocks all around him, below him, above him, underneath him. Suddenly it made sense.

The rocks were exercising! Of course! They were moving about, stretching themselves, changing positions. Maybe they were even speaking to each other, and this was the sound of stone language.

Anthony wondered why he had not thought of this before. He had long sensed a kind of magic about this heap of boulders and this explanation filled him with relief. He smiled at the thought of being a witness to the Boulders shifting and speaking. He could hardly wait to tell his parents.

He stood up, filled with the confidence that comes from solving a problem, and he edged himself around the nearest rocky shoulder.

Then he stopped. He closed his eyes tight and opened them wide. He inhaled an *O* of air, and his mouth froze in that gasp. For before him was an opening between the rocks—an opening in the rocks that was just large enough for Anthony. Like an invitation, this unexpected hole seemed meant just for him.

Maybe, just maybe, the Boulders were inviting him in.

CHAPTER 7

Crack, Split, Cleft...Portal!

Anthony stared at the opening. He'd been right! The boulders really had moved. They had stretched apart. This hole, this yawning mouth in the rocks, was proof.

He looked behind him, around him. Nothing else seemed to have changed. He wished his father would suddenly appear and together they could investigate this crack, a *cleft* his father might say. *Cleft* was one of Anthony's dictionary words that was also illustrated. His father had helped him with the drawing. Right now, if his father were here, he would remind Anthony to be careful. "Watch your step," he would say.

Anthony took several steps, watching each foot take him closer to the strange hole. Even from several yards away he could see it was a narrow opening, irregular in shape, maybe four feet tall, widest in the middle section. It appeared to follow the natural seams between the boulders, as if several great stones had simply separated cleanly, one from another. Nothing had broken apart. There were no rocky fragments lying about. There was something strangely natural about this split, this cleft in the rock.

This was a *portal!* A kind of entrance! Anthony's heart beat faster.

Anthony knew the word *portal*. It was #6 in his dictionary, and a cousin to *portcullis*, #5, his very favorite castle word.

Castle words...

For a few brief moments Anthony's memory transported him to another school day when Mrs. Quickett had asked the children to list all the castle words they could in two minutes. Only two minutes? Anthony could have written pages of castle words.

Turret, battlements, dungeon, portcullis...

When he had written *portcullis*, he paused, thinking about this amazing apparatus of defense and architecture. And in that pausing, he and his pencil left the path of the Assignment and began to sketch the heavy iron gridwork of a portcullis, a serious defense to entrance at a castle gate. Anthony was still designing his imagined portcullis when Mrs. Quickett called "Time!"

"It is a splendid portcullis, Anthony," Mrs. Quickett had said later when it was his time to share his list of just four words. "Do you think you were snagged by that portcullis, Anthony?" Mrs. Quickett had smiled when she said this. Anthony remembered that now.

Snagged by the portcullis.

Anthony stared again at the opening. He stepped closer. There was no portcullis here. He took another step, and now he could touch the edges of the opening. He ran his palms up and down, confirming what his eyes had already reported.

The stone edges felt smooth and almost polished, as if this were an ancient doorway. And there was something different about the light as it reflected from these stones bordering the entrance. There was no portcullis.

Anthony took another step. Now he could see a few feet within the opening, but only as far as the afternoon light traveled. Bending from the waist and bracing his hands on either side of the stony entrance, he stuck his head inside. It was really dark, for Anthony's upper body blocked much of the outside light. He knew his eyes would adjust, so he just waited in that bent position—eyes wide, ears on alert.

He took a deep breath of the heavy smell of stone, ancient and cold. Even from the entrance Anthony felt he was breathing air that had been sealed off, shut away within the earth. Maybe he was the first person to breathe this cold, stony air.

Could creatures be living inside this space? Cave creatures like bats or snakes . . . even bears? He listened. Nothing. He squinted his eyes. Gradually he saw a small cave with walls that curved up, like an upside-down bowl. No sign of bears. Anthony's eyes moved all around, up, down, left to right. It was just a rocky, empty chamber.

Then he saw it!

The airplane! Mrs. Quickett's note had somehow flown through the opening and landed on the other side of the cave.

Anthony could reach it in two or three steps, four steps at the most.

He pushed back from the cave entrance and looked around behind him. The sun was slipping away from this afternoon. Already this side of the Boulders lay in deep shadow. He just needed to step inside and get the airplane. Now.

Anthony took a deep breath, wiped his sweaty hands on his jeans, and wrinkled all of himself inside. It was a tight fit, and his body plugged up much of the hole, preventing light from seeping in around him.

It was so dark! It was a darkness stronger than the familiar darkness of his bedroom at night or the cozy darkness of his messy closet with the door closed. Anthony wondered if the very air were black.

He remembered another darkness within another hole. Recently his father had read *The Silver Chair* to him, and when they got to the scene where the children had to slip into the tight, dark hole to escape the giants, Anthony had crawled into his dad's lap. They finished that chapter, and later the whole book just like that, sharing the adventure in the comfort of the big green wingback chair in the living room.

"No giants here." Anthony's small voice surprised him. He wished for the company of his father right now. He wished to be sitting now in the green wingback chair and telling his parents about his adventures on this strange day.

"NO GIANTS HERE!" he repeated now in his capital-letter voice. Feeling with his hands for the stony edges of this tight passage through the darkness, Anthony twisted and squirmed forward as he repeated, "NO GIANTS HERE! NO GIANTS HERE!"

Those spoken words encouraged and strengthened Anthony, and soon he realized he had gotten through the narrow space, and he could stand up, tall and straight. Even extending his arms above him and all around him, he could not touch the roof or the sides of the passageway. The chamber was much larger than he had thought.

He stepped slightly to one side, hoping that the light he had blocked would now travel into this hollowed space and he would see the airplane. He looked behind him, but the opening showed pale with fading light from a setting sun. There was barely enough light to guide his exit. He turned back toward the cave.

Anthony took a deep breath of the inky air. There was no sound, no dripping water through limestone, no grinding of moving rocks, no rustlings or growlings of invisible creatures. Just the darkness. Nothing seemed to be inside this space except him, his airplane, and this darkness.

But darkness always brings questions, and as Anthony wondered what to do next, it occurred to him that he might be wrong about this cave. Perhaps he was intruding. Perhaps there was someone or something that did live within this heap of boulders...certainly not giants and maybe not bears, but something watching him now.

He said in a loud, clear voice, "Hello, Darkness! Hello! Hello, to anyone who hears me! I am Anthony. Anthony Bartholomew Mandopolis. I am a nine-year-old boy, and I have come inside to get my paper airplane. It flew accidentally into this cave." Anthony paused and took an especially big breath. "I am getting it now, and then I am leaving." Here he paused again, listening for any shift in the silence. "Good-bye," he said to the Silence and the Darkness, and because he was already grateful for the strength of his voice and the possible goodwill that existed even in such darkness, he added, "Thank you! Thank you very much!"

He resumed his slow, careful, hands-in-front walk across the dark space he hoped was still the cave, in the direction he imagined held his airplane. He spoke directly and aloud to himself, words that were full of purpose, words brightening with hope.

"This cave is empty, and I am safe," he said, taking a step forward. "There are no giants here. There are no bears, no snakes, not any kind of monster. I can walk straight ahead until my feet touch the airplane on the floor." He took a deep breath and another step forward and then another. "I must be very close to the airplane now. I will pick it up and hurry back to the outside and home again."

He swept his tennis shoes across the floor, listening, feeling for that soft rustle of paper. But something was happening. Something was changing.

Anthony stopped. He squinted his eyes. He opened them wide. Was he seeing his own hands outstretched? And there! There were his gray tennis shoes. They were standing on a stone floor. He watched as the darkness seemed to be swallowed by a swelling brightness. Within moments what had begun as faint light had grown into a radiant brilliance, illuminating a room of enormous size, a room dazzling with light.

And Anthony was standing right in the very middle of it.

CHAPTER 8

Light

L ight! Brilliant, golden light!

Anthony turned around and around again, watching as the light illuminated not a small cave room but an enormous cavern.

He was spellbound by the sight before him.

The floor was a *mosaic* of thick, heavy stones in shades of dark and light. He was standing on a large center stone, encircled by larger and larger rings of stones like petals in the zinnias of his mother's garden. From this centerpiece many stone pathways looped and spiraled away toward the cavern walls where they ended. No doorways, no dark entrances, no portals suggested any further passage beyond this enormous room.

Anthony gazed upward at the smooth, polished walls surrounding him. They reflected and ricocheted the growing light, multiplying the brilliance. He bent his small body backward to find the limits of this place, looking up, up and up.

Then he saw the lights! Hundreds—no, thousands—of lights shining from above.

"Stars! . . Stars?" Anthony frowned. "If those are really stars, then I must be outside. But I'm not outside. I'm inside this cave." All of this said in a whispery voice, followed by a long quiet pause as he thought about this puzzle above him.

Had the outside turned inside?

Anthony looked back at the stars. He knew about stars. He knew about *constellations* (#25 in his dictionary). His father had told him stories of the stars and how they guided travelers. Perhaps they could guide him now. He began to search for Polaris, the North Star.

"Polaris is the place to start." His father's words echoed back to him from a cold January night not so long ago.

They had climbed to the Nest of the Boulders in late afternoon and watched as the sun slipped behind a firework sky of purples, oranges, and golds. They had watched as the shadows lengthened and spread themselves out into a blanket of winter darkness. They had watched as porch lights and stoplights, bridge lights and shop lights, winked and blinked below them in Centerville, and as car headlights trailed off into the countryside. They had watched as the stars brightened one by one in the dark night sky. They had eaten peanut butter sandwiches and sipped cocoa from Anthony's brand new thermos, but mostly they had watched.

That night they had sighted Polaris, and Anthony had checked its position with his compass. From Polaris they had found both Dippers and, looking south, Orion. Anthony had been able to spot Rigel, his next favorite star. His father had retold the stories of Orion and Pegasus and Taurus, the bull. The night sky was like a book, his dad had said.

Now Anthony looked back up, searching for Polaris in the sky of this cave.

"Where is the North Star? Where..." He stopped. Suddenly he remembered his paper airplane and the reason he was now standing in this strange place with stars in the ceiling and light coming from everywhere around him. "The airplane!" He spoke aloud. He turned around, looking up and down the pathways for the airplane he had clearly seen from the cave entrance, just minutes ago. "I have plenty of light. Plenty of light. I can find it now."

However, while he was so occupied with this search, head to the ground, eyes scanning the patterned floor, something seemed to be happening above him. If he had just glanced up, he would have noticed that one particularly bright light had separated from the others and was growing larger and larger. It was traveling directly toward Anthony, though he did not realize this until he heard the whirring sound.

He looked up.

The whirring came from a spangly orb of light, about the size of a baseball, propelled by a multitude of transparent wings. The ball of light skidded to a stop in mid-air, so close to Anthony's face that he took a quick step backward, just to be safe, of course. But Anthony immediately sensed something good about this creature, even before it spoke in a breathless but formal voice, a voice full of greeting and cheer.

"Welcome, Anthony Bartholomew Mandopolis. Welcome!"

CHAPTER 9

Pteros Chronos

"Welcome, Anthony Bartholomew Mandopolis!" The orb of light repeated its welcome a little louder and flew a little closer.

Anthony stepped back again. He did not know how to respond. Though nothing about this strange light really frightened him, he had no experience with such a creature. He could not even see a face.

"Welcome to the Realm of Inner Time," the light continued. "I am Pteros Chronos of the Order Alpha, and I have the honor of serving as your guide throughout your journey here." The light took a quick gasp of air before continuing, "and I must apologize for arriving a little late." The orb of light pulsated and shimmered as it spoke, straining as one might do after a strenuous race, yet still maintaining a formality and a true spirit of hospitality.

Anthony juggled a sense of wonder with some uncertainty. That word 'journey' had caught him. A journey? With a light? Where? He was tired and hungry, and it was probably late. Time to be home.

But this light, this traveling and speaking light! Anthony searched for a mouth, even a face within this hovering, whirring mass of brilliance. The whirring, he realized, was caused by the rapidly moving wings. So many wings, translucent as dragonfly wings, encircled the light and beat at once, creating a gauzy whirlwind.

But a journey? He simply wanted to find his airplane and head home.

"Hello, sir . . . Mr. Guide . . . sir. I did not quite understand your name, sir." Anthony spoke hesitantly, unsure about addressing such a being, though certain of the importance of eye contact and first impressions.

The light seemed to take a breath, expanding itself into a cantaloupe-sized radiance and spoke more slowly in what Anthony recognized as a teaching voice.

"I am Pteros, spelled *P-T-E-R-O-S*, the *P* being silent. Like Teros. Pteros Chronos. It is a Greek name. Do you know any Greek, Anthony?"

"Yes, yes, I know some Greek." Anthony was instantly comforted by the mention of a familiar subject. He was thinking of Zeus, Poseidon, all the stories from the constellations, his yearning to be Icarus, and his *Big Book of Greek Myths* at home right now, under his bed and within easy reach.

"Well then," continued the light, "you will know what my name means. Pteros for winged, as in pterodactyl, that early flying reptile, extinct now in your kingdom. And Chronos ..."

"Yes!" Anthony yelled out, for he did know the answer. "Chronos for Time! It's like *chronology* in my spiral dictionary. It means 'things in order, just like they happened'!" Anthony smiled broadly, excited with this word game. He wondered if Mr. Trippett would be able to guess the meaning of Pteros Chronos—and this thought led him to a tiny flash of a memory when he stood with Mr. Trippett on Elm Street and talked about the wind and Far Away. He remembered Mr. Trippett's words, "Pay attention." He looked closely at this orb of glowing light, so near to him and speaking words he could understand.

"Well, yes indeed," said the whirring light. "You are a clever boy. Yes! Pteros Chronos means 'Winged Time' or 'Time Flying.' We think of ourselves as Time Flies." With this statement, the light brightened and zoomed around Anthony, sending glittery rays in all directions. It skidded once again quite close to Anthony's face. "You may call me PC if you wish, though I do not generally encourage abbreviations."

"I like your whole name, Mr. Pteros Chronos." Anthony gazed upward at the winking lights. "Those lights up there...are they all Time Flies? All of them?"

"Well, yes, though now they are in a kind of hibernation. They await assignments. But I am here now with you. You are my assignment."

Anthony was silent at this. After all, what sort of assignment could this luminous creature have with him, unless it had something to do with finding his airplane.

"Mr. Pteros Chronos, I need to find my airplane. It is really a note from my teacher. It accidentally flew into this place," and here Anthony's voice had a slight wobble to it, not unobserved by the Time Fly.

"Ah, yes. Mrs. Quickett. Yes. We know of her. Somewhat misguided, but earnest and kind." The light inflated and then deflated, balloon-like, and with a great sigh. "And to your question about my assignment, " here the light paused, then grew larger again, "yes. My assignment is Finding Anthony's Airplane. I am your guide and friend in that Finding." In a quieter voice he added, "though I do not believe the airplane's arrival here was due to accidental events. Nevertheless, I am to accompany you on your journey."

There it was again. The word 'journey.' Anthony's eyes brimmed with the tears that often accompany weariness and confusion. His voice caught in his throat, and his words stumbled out in sputters and sniffles.

"Please, Mr. Pteros Chronos...please. I really need to go home. My parents will be worried if I...I have to find it...my airplane...that note...it's my responsibility. There is plenty of light, but I...I can't find it," Anthony's small shoulders were shaking now. His face glistened with tears.

The light widened, encompassing all of Anthony.

"Oh, Anthony. Forgive me. I fear I have done this all wrong. It comes, I'm afraid, from my late arrival and feeling rushed and hurried." The light continued to encircle Anthony, spreading warmth and comfort. "Let me try to explain once again. You have been chosen, Anthony, especially chosen for this journey. And I have been chosen, too. We have been chosen to be a team. Together we will travel through Inner Time and together we will find your airplane. Here. I've brought you a light refreshment. I was warned that you might be hungry in this early stage of our journey." Pteros Chronos motioned to a small leather bag on the stone floor. It was lumpy and drawn together with strings. Anthony had not noticed it.

"What's this?" Anthony's voice remained wobbly.

"What would you like it to be, Anthony?"

Anthony looked again at this orb of shimmering, radiant light.

"Well, I'd like it to be...could it be a chocolate milkshake?"

"Certainly. Just give the bag a twirl, a spin, and make sure the string is tight, of course. A few twirls and you should be able to drink a milkshake right out of the bag...did you say chocolate?"

Anthony nodded and picked up the almost weightless bag, wondering that it could hold anything. He checked the strings and twirled it carefully. Holding it to his mouth, he was surprised when a chocolate milkshake, liquid and delicious, poured from the bag. It filled all the places inside him that needed filling.

"Thank you, Pteros Chronos, sir. That was a wonderful milkshake. I feel much better now." Anthony replaced the bag on the stone floor, wondering if it held hamburgers, too. "Should we take this bag with us?" Anthony had camped enough to know the importance of packing food and water for any journey.

"No need. We will be provisioned. And you are safe with me, Anthony. Well, mostly safe."

The light spoke these last three words in a whispery gush, which sounded more like an exhaled breath. Coupled with the hiccups left over from his sobbing and his gulping the milkshake, Anthony never heard them.

CHAPTER 10

Illusions

Anthony breathed in a big breath. He looked hard at this whirring, winged light with a Greek name, a light that had brought him a milkshake. It had so easily enlarged and encircled him. Now, as a baseball-size radiance, it hovered and beamed at eye level on his right. Could he trust it? And why was he, Anthony, chosen for this journey? Something had happened in that light-filled hug and in drinking that chocolate milkshake. Could the light have charged him in some magical way? He did feel brave once again, and not the least bit hungry. There was something good and hopeful about traveling with light.

"So, Mr. Pteros Chronos, sir, what should we do now?" Anthony's voice surprised him. Despite his questions, it was steady and sure.

"Well, yes. Now." The light pulsated a moment, then continued. "Now. You must choose a path. Any path will do. Just choose one, and we will begin. Now, go ahead."

Anthony looked again at the many paths that looped and spun off in haphazard directions from the stone center where he stood. He studied the stone walls where they all ended.

"But how do I know which is the right path? They don't go anywhere. They all just stop at the walls."

"Are you certain of that, my boy? Don't be fooled by *illusions*, Anthony. You do know about illusions don't you?"

Before Anthony could answer, Pteros Chronos spread himself out into a ribbon of golden light with waves that curled and crested and billowed like a luminous river. It circled around Anthony along the floor of the cavern as a glowing stream, and then quickly returned to its baseball size once again.

"Wow! How'd you do that?" Anthony made a mental note to add illusion to his spiral dictionary.

"We Time Flies are masters of illusion, Anthony. We materialize in many forms. Over the years I have attended you as candlelight on your birthday cake, the flashlight when you have hiked at night, moonlight through your window. Once I substituted a whole week as the nightlight in your bedroom. Just checking on you...from time to time. That's a phrase we Time Flies like to use."

"You've been assigned to me all my life?" Anthony frowned. How had he missed something so magical and so close to him all these years? He wondered if Mr. Trippett knew anything about Time Flies. Was that why he kept reminding Anthony to pay attention? "Were you...were you...ever a lightning bug in my backyard?" Anthony asked with hesitation, remembering last summer when he left a whole jar of lightning bugs under his bed. For too long.

"No, no, no," Pteros Chronos chuckled, sending a shower of light spangles all around Anthony. "Those creatures you call lightning bugs are born of beetles. We come from the dust of light years. Though certainly lightning bugs serve a purpose. They are lovely on a summer night, and, I am told, they are quite delicious if you are a bat. But we Time Flies carry a different sort of light, heavenly in nature. No, no, we are not even distantly related." The light paused for a moment, allowing the importance of his words to sink in with Anthony. "Now, Anthony. Choose"

Anthony did. He chose the looping path on his right, the path just under where Pteros Chronos whirred and hovered. He stepped out of the circle, Pteros Chronos a few beats behind him, and walked on the strange curving path leading to the cavern wall.

As he neared the solid wall, he slowed. Was this an illusion, or was he going to boink his nose?

"Just keep walking," whispered Pteros Chronos.

Trusting the light, Anthony walked on. Somehow the stone wall accepted Anthony's nose and arms and feet and knees, swallowing up the whole of Anthony in a kind of rippling tickle. Pteros Chronos followed.

CHAPTER 11

Advice for the Journey

In just a wink of time, Anthony found he was standing on a dirt path at the edge of a grassy meadow, mostly circular in shape. A thick forest of great trees encircled the clearing, and overhead the sky stretched out in shades of blue and purple.

"Wow! Look, Mr. Pteros Chronos! Look! We're in a forest! We're outside!" But to himself, Anthony half whispered, "At least I think this is outside."

Indeed it did look like outside. It felt like outside. Though after the Time Fly's demonstration of illusions, Anthony was not sure.

Turning all around and then around again, Anthony saw that the trail wound through the trees behind him and continued beyond him up a small hill where it disappeared from view. He heard birdsong, and in the corner of his eye caught the quick dash movement of squirrels playing chase in the upper branches of a nearby pine. The woodsy smell of old trees after a recent rain traveled on a light breeze. Anthony took a big breath of the wide open outside.

There was no heap of huge boulders or any sign of a stone wall. Anthony knew he had not walked on the dirt path trailing behind him. There were no footprints in the soft damp dirt.

"Do illusions have smells and noises? Can you touch an illusion, Mr. Pteros Chronos?"

Anthony bent near the wheat-colored grass edging the path. Tiny beads of rain had collected on the seed heads and reflected the sunlight. He gently swept his hand through the wet grass, scattering a sprinkling of diamonds.

He had been so focused on the scene before him, so grateful to be amid trees and under a blue sky, even if all of this was an illusion, that Anthony had momentarily forgotten about his guide. During that time, Pteros Chronos had both dimmed and distanced himself.

Anthony was immediately alarmed. Even the Time Fly's whirring was faint.

"Is something wrong? Are you all right, Mr. Pteros Chronos?"

"Oh, yes, quite all right, Anthony. Intentional dimming. Sometimes it's best that I disappear. Your travel through this clearing is being closely monitored. My presence will not be of any help to you here. In fact, we Time Flies try to avoid this particular zone altogether. We seem to be agitations to the local official."

"Agitations?" Anthony's voice grew small. He was uneasy. Pteros Chronos was vanishing before his eyes.

"You know, my boy. Nuisances, bothers, irritations. It would be best not to even mention our friendship. But, do ask about your airplane. It's quite possible you will learn something of its whereabouts. Now, pay attention."

"But, do I have to go without you?" There was the slightest hint of returning wobbles in his throat as he spoke these words. Anthony glanced again at the path leading up and over the hill to whatever lay beyond.

"Anthony, you are thoroughly able to walk up the hill and down it again. You are equipped to meet whomever you may meet and exchange pleasantries, even information. I will wait for you at that far end of the clearing where those tallest trees gather around the dirt track. I will be disguised as sunshine on the branches. Do you think you can identify me when I appear as sunshine?" Here Pteros Chronos paused, waiting for the nod that told him Anthony understood.

Pteros Chronos was just a faint glow now, reminding Anthony of an ember floating and swirling from a campfire. Even his voice was vanishing. But he continued. "I have but a few suggestions for your journey, Anthony."

The Time Fly had now completely disappeared. Even the whirring had stopped. Directions came to Anthony as if borne by the breeze. He was not sure if he was actually hearing the words spoken or if he had simply absorbed them from the air around him. However they came, they remained three uncommonly good suggestions for all his journeys in the years that followed. He would later write them down just as he remembered them, storing them under his bed in a small velvet-lined jewelry box that belonged to his mother.

1. Travel lightly—you have everything you need within you.

2. Travel expectantly—you will discover more than your airplane.

3. Travel kindly—you will find kindness always returns to the sender.

Anthony waited just a bit, thinking about all that Pteros Chronos had said and watching for sunshine to appear on those faraway trees, now holding shadows. He hoped to see a signal, something telling him that Pteros Chronos had arrived there and waited for him. But the trees remained dark and unchanged for the moment. Perhaps they were just too distant.

Still Anthony trusted his guide would be there when he arrived. All he had to do was walk over the hill and through the clearing on the other side. He had everything he needed right inside of him. Pteros Chronos had told him so.

CHAPTER 12

High Time

The dirt path zigzagged gently up the hillside. It was an easy climb, the day was perfect for hiking, and Anthony felt brave and strong. Each switchback (his father's word for this kind of looping trail) brought him closer to the hilltop where he hoped he might see distant mountains or a shining sea—or his airplane. So far, the higher he climbed, the farther the forest stretched green to the horizon.

Pteros Chronos had said he had all he needed, but Anthony soon wished for his real hiking boots with the neon green laces and the gripping soles. And that idea led to another wish—his canvas backpack. It was packed for camping and filled with a flashlight with extra batteries, twenty feet of rope, his compass, small first aid kit with bandages and tiny tweezers, and three distress signal flares for emergencies.

Anthony looked back up at the crest of the hill, considering just where he would set off those flares to achieve the most visibility. That is, should he need to, and if he had the flares. Then he saw something that made him stop. Just over the hill, rising from that invisible downside, was the top of a structure. A tower maybe? It was hard to tell from where Anthony stood, for the remaining hilltop hid most of it. Whatever it was, it looked old, and it shimmered in the sunlight.

Anthony walked a little faster. Turning on the next switchback, with his eyes fixed on the increasingly larger object, which by now seemed most definitely to be a tower, he almost missed a small white sign half hidden at the grassy edge of the path. It read:

High Time

Arrival Time: 2 Minutes

An arrow pointed straight up the hill.

Two minutes! Anthony counted the remaining switchbacks. There were four. He'd need to hurry.

Anthony walked fast. Then faster. Two minutes meant just 120 seconds, and he didn't want to begin his journey by being late. Though he did wonder just a bit about who might be keeping time.

Even when he heard the sounds, he didn't pause. They were familiar, mechanical sounds—tapping, clicking, ticking. He had heard them before, but where? When?

As he hurried, his view of the tower grew and so did the strength of the sounds, until Anthony, now panting, finally reached the top of the hill. Here the path led under an ancient stone archway quite covered with curling vines. The words *High Time* were barely visible in a weathered sign dangling and squeaking from a rusty hook near the top of the arch. Anthony passed through the archway.

"Ohhhhhh," he sighed. Now he could see the whole tower. It was a spectacular sight, unlike anything he had ever even imagined.

An octagonal clock tower stood very tall itself, but it was taller still because it stood on a high wooden platform. A narrow flight of stairs spanned the airy distance between the ground and a front door. Covering the tower, like a mosaic on all the sides and right up to the pointed roof, were clocks! All sorts and all sizes of clocks—big grandfather clocks, digital clocks, pendulum clocks, tiny pocket watches, round school clocks, mantle clocks, small wristwatches, travel clocks, small alarm clocks, and even cuckoo clocks—all ticking, tocking, clicking, chiming, buzzing, and dinging at the same time.

That was the sound! Anthony stood still and listened to this very noisy racket of measured and marked minutes. The clocks spoke in separate voices, and none of them told the same time. It was a strange chorus.

A low fence pinched the tower into a small, bare yard where no grass grew. There were no trees, no flowerbeds, no bird feeders or lawn furniture. And no sign of the airplane. The brown ground seemed beaten and hard, and Anthony wondered about the need for a fence at all on such an open hilltop.

He walked closer to the fence to get a better look. It served more as a boundary marker, for it was too small to keep anyone in or out. Made of small wooden blocks, pyramid in shape and linked together, it looked like a circle of children joining hands. Each pyramid waved a metal arm, clicking and clacking, back and forth, and, like the clocks above, each marked time to a different beat.

"Metronomes?" Anthony's question was lost in the noise around him. "Metronomes!" he repeated to himself, suddenly thinking of Miss Zingit, his piano teacher. Miss Viola Zingit (though he had never spoken her first name aloud) had taught him about metronomes, showing him the one she was given one Christmas when she was about his age.

"It keeps time as you play, Anthony," she had said.

Anthony wondered then about where that wooden pyramid kept the time, and if he could just open the inside to see the special place where Time was kept. And would Time be surprised at being discovered, hiding away in this special wooden box?

He would tell Miss Zingit about this fence, made of little metronomes and the clock tower. He would tell her how much he loved coming to her house on Wednesdays after school and sitting with her at the piano. He would practice more. He would tell her that, too, when he...

Suddenly Anthony remembered that Pteros Chronos was waiting for him. He would want to know if Anthony had discovered any news of the airplane. Anthony needed to see if anyone at High Time could help him. He would do that now. Right now.

He looked back up at the front door of the clock tower. There was no sign of anyone inside. But, all these clocks and the metronomes? Who did all this winding? Now Anthony noticed an ancient hourglass just inside the fence on one side of the front walk. The last grains of silvery sand emptied through the narrow waist and onto the large heap of sand collecting in the bottom. Whose job was it to turn over this heavy hourglass?

Anthony looked at the wooden steps leading up to the door.

Pteros Chronos had told him to travel expectantly.

Now was the time. He would knock on the front door. He would expect someone to answer. He would expect that someone to be someone who would help him find his airplane.

CHAPTER 13

Mr. E. Exactus Watchit

Anthony climbed carefully. The handrail was loose and jangly, and several steps were broken or missing altogether.

When he reached the top of the platform and faced the front door, he could better see the clocks and the sad condition of the clock tower. The clock faces were grimy, their numbers faded, their metal fixtures badly rusted. A grey bucket stood near the door, filled with old batteries, wire, and partially used tubes of contact cement. Several cuckoos were missing wings, a few of the pendulums had broken, and, even though the clocks continued to click and tick out the time, there was a tiredness to their sound.

Taped to the door was a faded, handwritten sign, which Anthony squinted to read.

Mr. E. Exactus Watchit

Proprietor, Executor and Official Time Keeper

Please Knock

The word *Loudly* was written across the sign in a darker ink and was the only clearly visible word. *Loudly* seemed to state the obvious, considering all of the ticking clocks.

Anthony knocked. Loudly.

Immediately he heard a loud thud as if something heavy had fallen inside the tower. Rustling noises and rapid footsteps followed the thud. Somewhere a door creaked and then creaked again. There were more rapid footsteps, now coming right to the front door. A pause. A clearing of a throat.

The door opened.

A very tall man stood within the doorframe. He wore tall, shiny, black lace-up boots, with squared and clunky heels that alone were five inches high. Stuffed inside the boots were the generous baggy legs of brown trousers made of a coarse cloth. Pockets were attached up and down the fronts of these pants and into all of these pockets golden chains disappeared, attached, Anthony guessed, to pocket watches. The man wore a safari hat and thin, wire-rimmed glasses, and his black-and-white striped shirt made him look like the soccer officials at Anthony's Saturday games. But the shirt was wrinkled and untucked and had not been properly buttoned so that one extra buttonhole dangled at his waist, and the extra button crowded up under the man's throat. In the time it took Anthony to look at him from boots to hat, the man did not move or seem to even notice the small boy below his line of vision. He continued to stand in the door frame and peer outside without lowering his head.

"Hello," ventured Anthony.

When the man looked down, Anthony was caught immediately by his quick blue eyes. Magnetic blue eyes that danced about in a long face that held little other expression. His forehead was long, his nose was pointed and long, his ears were exaggerated and drooped, and his chin tapered to a point that, when lowered, seemed to collide with his chest.

"Oh! There you are," said the man. "I am not accustomed to visitors. Especially visitors at this time of day," he paused, bending closer and looking carefully at Anthony. "Especially small visitors," he added.

The man stepped outside the doorway and onto the platform, straightened himself to an even taller height, cleared his throat and spoke in such rapid talk Anthony had to concentrate to keep up with him.

"I am E. Exactus Watchit. The E. stands for Evermore. I am official Time Keeper of High Time and all surrounding Grassy Meadowlands. I am responsible for Taking Up Your Time. Do you have any Time to hand over? You need to make it quick. You will be completely out of Time soon. You could possibly end up in Time Out. Quickly, hand it over." And then he gasped, completely out of breath, with his palm outstretched in Anthony's direction.

Anthony frowned. This sounded like a memorized speech, and besides, had Pteros Chronos said anything about handing over Time? Anthony pursed his lips together and tried to remember the directions.

Mr. Watchit was tapping his foot on the wooden floor, checking the time on his several pocket watches and looking around as one does when impatiently waiting for someone to do something.

"I don't understand, Mr. Watchit. I am just traveling through the meadow. I am just looking for my paper airplane. I flew it off the Boulders and lost it. I thought you might have seen it."

There was a long pause as Mr. Watchit worked his mouth in what seemed to Anthony to be warm-up exercises.

"I see, I see," he finally said, his eyes flitting about and ending up on Anthony. He leaned closer. "Your airplane, you say? Do you mean to say that you have no Time on your hands? Nothing to hand over to me? Do you understand that I am extremely busy? Winding, setting, logging, checking," he paused briefly to take a breath. "All of this takes my Time. I have no Time to spare. I certainly have no Time to investigate lost airplanes!" Again Mr. Watchit took a big gasp of air. He had been talking so fast, that it seemed he had somewhat deflated. He looked as if he had actually become a little smaller.

"No, sir. I have no Time on my hands. I am actually here because I have a little problem with Time." Anthony told Mr. Watchit the whole story of Mrs. Quickett's note, his trying to fly from the Boulders, meeting Pteros Chronos in the strange cave, and finally how he had ended up here at High Time. He blurted the part about Pteros Chronos, forgetting the Time Fly's warning.

Mr. Watchit seemed unaffected by the mention of Anthony's guide. He had sat down on the platform floor halfway through the story. His hat had fallen off, exposing even more of his tall forehead, which crested into a very bald head. He listened to Anthony's story with great interest, often gazing off, over the meadow below and the green forest beyond, a faraway look in his shining blue eyes.

"And so that's why I am here now, with you. I am still looking for the airplane," Anthony said. "I was hoping that maybe you would have some news of it."

Mr. Watchit didn't respond. It seemed he was transported to a place far beyond the grassy meadow. Anthony knew the look.

"Do you, Mr. Watchit?"

"Do I?"

"Do you know anything about my paper airplane?"

"Well, well, well. Indeed. News of your lost airplane. I suppose I could check my schedule of Arrivals and Departures. Hmm...," and now Mr. Watchit looked directly at Anthony and began again to answer rapidly. "Trouble with Time you say. Well, yes! I do know about that. I, too, have a little problem with time. I *do* have Time on my hands, too much Time. And it is all on *my* hands, don't you see, Anthony? It's all about Time.

"I am responsible for all of this, for Keeping Time, Measuring Time, Checking the Time. And all of these Clocks! All the winding. There is no Time to stop. I shouldn't be talking with you now. No Time to visit and tell stories, no Time for tea and crackers, no Time to watch sunsets and write poetry. And no Time to search for lost airplanes. No. No Time at all."

With a great upheaval of legs and arms, Mr. Watchit stood up, replaced his safari hat, spoke a quick good-bye, and closed the door, leaving Anthony outside and alone.

CHAPTER 14

Leaving High Time

Anthony sat very still. The wind had picked up, and the platform groaned and creaked. It was suddenly cooler as the sun disappeared behind a bank of clouds, and a sad feeling settled over the hilltop. Anthony felt it. He zipped up his jacket.

He was unsure about what to do next. Mr. Watchit had disappeared into the clock tower, but Anthony couldn't just leave without saying good-bye. He felt sorry for Mr. Watchit. All the winding. All these clocks. All of this keeping up, none of which seemed to be going well.

He was still just sitting when he heard a new sound, quiet and muffled, through the door. Even with all the ticking of the clocks Anthony recognized the sound. Someone was crying.

He knocked on the door.

Silence.

He knocked again.

There were shuffling noises, which Anthony guessed to be Mr. Watchit collecting himself.

The door opened. Mr. Watchit stood again in the doorway, looking not nearly so tall as before. Anthony realized he had removed his boots and his safari hat. His eyes were red. His nose was red. He was trying to disguise the sniffles.

"Yes?" Mr. Watchit's voice was clogged and nasal.

"Mr. Watchit, sir, I am very sorry to bother you, sir. But I was wondering..." Anthony paused, but the words of that question actually began to spill out before Anthony had fully formed the question in his mind or considered possible answers much less the wisdom of such a question in the first place.

"I was just wondering, sir...if you might consider coming along...with me and Pteros Chronos?" Anthony paused again, watching for some signal that Mr. Watchit considered the Time Fly an unpleasant traveling companion.

Mr. Watchit's blue eyes watched the airy distance.

"We could use your skills, Mr. Watchit," Anthony continued quickly. "You would be another set of eyes, our best eyes. I know you would be a great help in finding my airplane. Must you really stay here, keeping time? I mean, I know this is a very important job, Mr. Watchit, but could you possibly leave it for a bit, just give the clocks a rest, too, just temporarily? Take some time off, Mr. Watchit."

A long pause followed. Anthony waited.

Mr. Watchit continued gazing out the doorway at some faraway place even beyond the green forest. His blue eyes were fixed and steady. His stillness was interrupted only by the occasional need to blow his nose with a red bandana he withdrew from one of his pockets.

Finally he looked back at Anthony. His eyes were soft, and his words traveled slowly and gently. "For years and years I've remained right here, on this hilltop, Anthony. Since I arrived here, as a young man, I have never even ventured down the hill. I was assigned to this station because I was the best in my class at accurate measurement—at the Royal Academy of Time Keeping, I'm sure you've heard of it—and highly skilled in mechanics. I have always been a responsible sort of fellow, reliable, trustworthy in every way. I caught the eye of my teacher, a professor of Ordinary Time, quite renowned in his field, though now I cannot recall his name or even what he looked like. I cannot remember much of that school, now that I think back. I am thoroughly knowledgeable with timepieces of every sort, with schedules and calculations, with ancient calendars and moon phases, but I am sadly unschooled in the world beyond this hilltop. I have no experience as a traveler, having never been on a trip, except to right here, High Time. That trip was a long time ago, Anthony. I do not even know how one travels."

Anthony was quiet. He had heard Mr. Watchit use that word 'responsible' and he felt an immediate connection. Mr. Watchit would understand why he must find his airplane. Being responsible was something he understood. But he also knew that Mr. Watchit had said something else remarkable and personal to him. Anthony took some time before he responded.

"Well, Mr. Watchit, I think you would be a perfect companion. A companion is a friend, and you don't need lessons in being a friend. Besides, you have so many skills that would be of help to us. You would be our best eyes in searching for my airplane. And, if something breaks, well, then you can fix it. I hope you'll say yes, Mr. Watchit."

There was another long pause. Anthony waited. He knew that he had just proposed something unimaginable and scary and exciting, and he knew that Mr. Watchit was considering it.

Suddenly Mr. Watchit turned and, looking directly at Anthony, said, "How would one go about it? Leaving a place such as this? I'm not sure how to do that."

"Well, I think you could pack up a few things, but not too much. We need to travel lightly. And you could put those things in a bag. I think you would maybe write a note for whoever might happen to come to High Time, explaining that you have taken some time off.

We could tape it to the front door. Then you'd just walk down the hill with me. It'll be easy, Mr. Watchit."

And so it was. Quite easy.

Mr. Watchit led Anthony inside the dark clock tower. He cleared a pile of heavy books off a chair, apologized for the mess and the dust, and said he'd be just a few minutes, packing up the necessary things for the trip. He disappeared behind a curtained doorway, and soon Anthony heard the sounds of packing. A door creaked, drawers opened and closed, a chair was scooted across the floor, and, best of all, a humming song accompanied all this activity behind the curtain.

In little time Mr. Watchit returned wearing a bright green Hawaiian shirt with blue and red toucans and carrying a worn brown leather traveling bag. He had replaced his tall black boots with red high-top sneakers, and his safari hat sat on his head. His blue eyes were hardly visible behind leather aviator goggles, but his face was filled with the light that comes from a deep smile.

After they taped a note to the door, Mr. Watchit took a moment to walk around the clock tower, inspecting and assessing all the clocks and the metronomes one last time.

Anthony watched. He knew Mr. Watchit was saying good-bye.

CHAPTER 15

Rendezvous

Anthony had been right. Leaving was easy for Mr. Watchit. It was Anthony who wished for more time in High Time.

He lagged behind Mr. Watchit as they headed down the hillside. He was not thinking about meeting Pteros Chronos under the tall trees. He was not even thinking about finding his airplane. He was thinking about that clock tower. He was thinking of all those books stacked on shelves that rose to the ceiling, books piled all over the floor and on tables and even on the only chair in the room. He was thinking of that strange gadget in the corner with pulleys and levers. He was thinking of the poster of Albert Einstein and an old, curled black-and-white photograph of Stonehenge taped to a drafting table. He was thinking of the charts and maps and schedules and ledgers and the hanging mobile of the solar system, and all of this covered in dust in a windowless tower where the only light came from a single bulb dangling on a thin wire.

The sound of Mr. Watchit's voice interrupted Anthony's remembering. Apparently he had been speaking for some time. Anthony now saw that he had stopped walking and was binocular-scanning the area below.

"And there. I see it. Aren't we supposed to *rendezvous* with Pteros Chronos among those trees down there?" Mr. Watchit was pointing downhill with a long finger.

Rendezvous? What was that? Anthony was unsure of the word. Did Mr. Watchit want to fight? Did this word have something to do with pistols or swords?

"Rendezvous?" Anthony asked.

"Well, I recall your saying that we were to meet in the tall trees nearest the path. Rendezvous means a meeting, usually between two people at a certain spot, at a certain time. I see the spot now. Clearly. Would you like to look through the binoculars?"

Anthony was relieved. Later he would add rendezvous to his dictionary, though it was several years before he would get the spelling right. He took the binoculars from Mr. Watchit, adjusted them to fit his eyes, and marveled at the close-up view of the pine needles from such a distance.

"Oh, yes. We are to meet Pteros Chronos right there. I do see the spot. He said he would be disguised as sunshine on the branches, but I don't see." Anthony's voice trailed off when he remembered that Pteros Chronos would be disguised so that Mr. Watchit would not recognize him. He glanced quickly at Mr. Watchit to see if he had heard him.

He had.

"Ah, yes," said Mr. Watchit with a faint smile. "Of course, a disguise. Time Flies are quite creative in their disguises. I myself have been fooled a time or two. They are remarkable creatures, really..." Then in a quieter voice, almost as if he were speaking to himself, Mr. Watchit said, "I fear I have not always treated them with respect or kindness." He paused.

"You see, they are so mobile, so quick to disappear, so acrobatic, so free, and, up until now, right now, I have been so immobile, so stuck, so imprisoned, really. I suppose it was envy, though I do hate to admit that. I wished to experience their freedom. For years I have wanted to fly away, too." Mr. Watchit sighed a long sigh.

"Though I think perhaps I have flown away just now, in a manner of speaking," he chuckled quietly. "Just this walking downhill. I have flown far enough to be very grateful that you came to High Time when you did, Anthony. It's quite strange really, but I feel a bit light myself. Perhaps I could try flying to Far Away too, as you did."

Anthony smiled back at this new friend whose face seemed to have relaxed into one easy smile after another.

"I do regret some of my behavior toward the Time Flies," continued Mr. Watchit. "Do you suppose, Anthony, that Pteros Chronos will accept me as a traveling companion?"

"Of course he will, Mr. Watchit, and he will be happy that you and I are friends." Anthony felt relief about the upcoming meeting of the three of them. He had not known Pteros Chronos long, but he was certain the Time Fly would not hold on to grudges.

When they reached the spot under the trees, the day had become chilly. The dense trees ahead loomed large and dark, and there was no sign of sunlight on the branches above them.

"I think this is a perfect spot for a cup of tea, while we await the arrival of Pteros Chronos," suggested Mr. Watchit as he removed a strange metal contraption from his traveling bag. It had short folding legs, which supported a plate-like platform and several mirrors attached by wires. He angled these mirrors to catch any remaining sunlight. Quickly he adjusted the height of the metal legs, placed twigs and dried leaves underneath, and set a blue enamel teapot on top of the platform. It was obviously a handmade burner, and though Anthony had never seen anything like it before, he was mostly interested in watching Mr. Watchit. His movements were swift and delicate and gentle, and he hummed to himself as he worked. Almost magically a small blaze bloomed and caught, and the teapot atop the little burner steamed with the comfort of something warm to drink.

"I always enjoy a cup of tea in the afternoon," he said, as he spread a faded yellow tablecloth on the ground and busied about with two little tin cups and green-fringed napkins. "But this occasion is particularly special. Today I am enjoying tea with you, my new friend. Well, indeed," he added shyly, "my best friend. I want to celebrate. I have oatmeal and prunes for our celebration."

Anthony's eyes widened. Oatmeal and prunes? This, too, in the traveling bag?

Mr. Watchit removed several small and carefully wrapped and labeled packages from the brown bag. Beyond oatmeal and prunes, there was brown sugar, toasted walnuts, a tin of crackers, and a small thermos of cream, which he poured into a tiny white pitcher.

Anthony politely declined the oatmeal and prunes, but the tea was a delicious raspberry and chamomile blend, and though the crackers were a little stale, he ate four. Mr. Watchit prepared his oatmeal as though this tea party were a ceremony, and even though Anthony never liked oatmeal, he never forgot the care Mr. Watchit took in its preparation.

The two of them sat at the forest's edge enjoying a picnic in the tender light of late afternoon and awaiting the arrival of Pteros Chronos. They were quiet with their own thoughts as both looked back at the hill they had just traveled down and at the clock tower standing all alone atop the platform at High Time.

Then, just as Anthony started to ask Mr. Watchit about the burner contraption, a familiar whirring sound interrupted their silence. Turning back to face the forest, they saw a shining orb spreading itself into rays of golden sunlight that slanted and pierced the branches above them in a spangly brilliance.

The rendezvous was accomplished.

CHAPTER 16

The Meantimes

A nthony and Mr. Watchit stared as rays of sunlight danced and splintered through the pine branches, gathering into a whirling orb of light that zoomed in and out among the trees. They smiled together, recognizing Pteros Chronos, disguised. It was spellbinding, a dazzling light show at the very least. Anthony wanted to clap, but he wondered if that would be *appropriate*. Appropriate was a word he had recently added to his dictionary. It was his grandmother's word, and she used it often.

They continued to sit and watch in silence as the Time Fly perched on the corner of the yellow tablecloth, his carefully folded wings disappearing into his brilliant light. He was close enough for them to see that he was winded, his deep breathing replacing the sound of whirring wings.

"Very nice to see you here with Anthony, Mr. Watchit," said Pteros Chronos, finally catching his breath. He spoke cheerfully. "Are you taking a holiday? I don't ever recall seeing you this far away from High Time."

"Well, yes, I suppose you could say that. A holiday, perhaps. Hmm...some time off? You see...I...I...we ll...Anthony..." Mr. Watchit stumbled about, trying to find the words to explain his presence. He glanced uneasily at Anthony.

"I've invited him! I've invited him to come with us!" Anthony said with a gush, wishing he had spoken up sooner and saved Mr. Watchit from such an awkward moment. "Mr. Watchit is going to join us in our search, Pteros Chronos."

"A splendid idea! I wish I had thought of it myself. Welcome, Mr. Watchit! We are glad to have your company and your help!" Pteros Chronos spoke with enthusiasm. "We are engaged in a serious search for Anthony's airplane—though I am sure he's shared that story with you."

"Yes, he has, and he is fortunate to have you as a guide. I hope to be of assistance as well. I've packed my gear, things I thought we might need on our journey," said Mr. Watchit, motioning to the traveling bag. "Though as you know, Pteros Chronos, I am not experienced as a traveler and...Oh! Forgive me, I have forgotten my manners with such excitement. Would you care for a cup of tea, Pteros Chronos?"

For another hour the three travelers visited together like old friends. There was no talk of past problems. They didn't discuss hurt feelings or boundary issues or misunderstood pranks. Both seemed happy to be connected by Anthony and the search for his airplane. Anthony was never to learn the nature of the past trouble between them. He never asked.

While Anthony helped Mr. Watchit extinguish the small fire and pack up the picnic supplies in the traveling bag, Pteros Chronos explained the reason for his late arrival. He had been detained by the Meantimes.

"Ahhhhhh...the Meantimes," said Mr. Watchit, looking up and smiling at Pteros Chronos. "I so enjoyed their visits to High Time. They drifted up quite regularly, so often that I sometimes imagined seeing them float by...a product of my loneliness, I suspect." There was a slight pause in his remembering. "Yes, I did...well, I do...I will...always I will enjoy my time with the Meantimes. They were, that is, they *are* a great comfort to me."

Anthony watched Mr. Watchit closely. His bright blue eyes were visible now that he had pocketed the aviator goggles. Those blue eyes seemed to be searching to understand this new time for him, this Now Time that wasn't run by clocks.

"Yes, yes," Mr. Watchit continued in a faraway voice, "I found the Meantimes to be quite thoughtful and wonderful times. I regret the reputation they suffer. Certainly there is nothing *mean* about them, as this word can suggest a shabbiness, a stinginess, a lowness of character. They are often treated with disregard, as if they are times of least importance, as if they carried emptiness around in a sack."

"Emptiness in a sack." Anthony repeated that to himself. He tried to imagine the sort of creatures who would carry emptiness in a sack. He wondered if he had ever read about them in books, but looking up, he found Pteros Chronos bobbing up and down and whirring loudly, which Anthony understood to mean he was ready to begin. He would ask about the Meantimes later.

"I suggest we establish a traveling order," said Pteros Chronos, eager to begin his role as guide. "I will lead us with my light low to the ground, allowing you to watch your step, Anthony. You should come after me, and then Mr. Watchit, you at the end with that miner's headlight, which I must say is a nifty device indeed."

And so it was that they arranged themselves in this order and began to walk through the thick trees and the growing darkness on the only path leading into the forest. There had been no discussion of waiting until morning to travel, though it seemed late to

Anthony to begin their journey with night so close. He had secretly wished to remain by the fire all night, listening to Mr. Watchit tell stories about High Time and the Meantimes, but traveling in complete darkness appeared to be quite natural for a glowing Time Fly who intended to stay on schedule.

The forest closed in around them, but the three progressed as if in a moving bubble of light. On and on they walked, climbing low hills, crossing dark streams, stepping over rocks, and keeping to the path. Buzzing sounds of cicadas, the ribbits of frogs, the occasional questionings of owls, and a soft wind ruffling the tree-tops filtered through the dark spaces around their moving light.

From time to time Anthony and Pteros Chronos waited while Mr. Watchit studied a night crawling forest beetle or touched the velvet drape of mossy rocks or stopped to listen to shufflings off in the dark. They stopped quite suddenly when Mr. Watchit, now wearing night-vision goggles and carrying his worn bird book, cried out at spotting a rare bald-headed Shusher Bird perched in upper branches of a nearby tree.

"Truly an amazing sight," he whispered, grateful the Shusher Bird had not been alarmed by his outburst. "All of this...truly amazing."

To which the Shusher Bird responded with its characteristic, "Shhhhh, shhhhhh, shhhhhhh."

Anthony tried very hard not to giggle while Mr. Watchit recorded the sighting in his bird book.

Mostly they traveled quietly, allowing each of them time to think. Anthony wondered again about the Meantimes and if his mother or father had ever met them. And what about Mrs. Quickett? Had she ever seen them carrying emptiness in a sack? Was this sack a backpack? Had they ever come into their classroom? Had he missed them? He decided to ask about them now.

"Excuse me, Mr. Pteros Chronos, sir, and Mr. Watchit, but exactly who are the Meantimes?"

It was Pteros Chronos who answered first. "Well, Anthony, I am guessing that you have already met the Meantimes. Perhaps you did not recognize them as such. Often this oversight is simply a result of inadequate language."

Anthony was not certain what "inadequate language" meant, but he sensed this was not a compliment.

"Certainly he has encountered them," offered Mr. Watchit from behind. "And certainly he has used those times in creative ways."

"You see, Anthony, it is often a matter of correct naming," continued the Time Fly, speaking in his teaching voice again, turning to face Anthony. (Though Anthony was never able to see his face, he always did his best to look directly at Pteros Chronos when he spoke.)

"Naming them with Proper Language," he continued. "Yes! That's the thing! You must think of the Meantimes as Whens. They are not Whos, and they are not Whats. They are Whens, moments that come to us between happenings—from time to time. And because they hold Time between events, they are often ignored, belittled, or left entirely unobserved."

Anthony wanted to stop walking and just talk about these amazing Meantimes. They seemed so important, and he wanted to recognize them when they came his way. But he was confused. Would a When have a face? Would a When speak outright or just whisper messages in your ear? He paused and turned back to see Mr. Watchit smiling.

"I like to think of them as intermissions, Anthony, like in a play. You've been to a play before?" Anthony nodded, remembering when he saw *A Christmas Carol* with his parents in December. For a moment his memory pulled him back into that dark theater downtown with the heavy maroon curtains and his mother's perfume and the tight shoes he had to wear. "Like those intermissions," Mr. Watchit smiled, waiting for Anthony to return from the memory to the conversation. "Like those intermissions, the Meantimes provide time to stretch and refresh oneself—to consider the events which have happened and to predict events to come. These Meantimes come to us quite full of enjoyment."

"And possibilities, Anthony, many possibilities," added Pteros Chronos, "though now I must change the subject. We are shortly close to a decision and one you must make, Anthony." He spoke as one might do, over a shoulder, though as an orb he did not have shoulders to speak over.

The group stopped once again, and Pteros Chronos turned to face them. He expanded in size and brilliance, Anthony guessed to signify the importance of his words, but possibly just to stretch a bit.

"In less than a mile we will reach what is known in these parts as Almost Hill. There the path splits, one path heading east, the other angling northwest. You will need to select a route, Anthony. I encourage you to give some thought to your selection." With that Pteros Chronos turned and began to whir and beam along the path again.

"Another strange choice to make," Anthony thought to himself, wondering how one should make a decision with such little information. But he thought as he walked and he walked as he thought until finally he spoke aloud, causing the group to halt once again.

"I have made my decision, Mr. Pteros Chronos, sir. Since I don't know enough about either path and nothing at all about Almost Hill, I think I will just wait until we get there. Then I can look for clues. I can listen. Maybe you and Mr. Watchit will give me advice. That's what I want to do." Anthony paused and then he smiled and said, "I decided all of that during the meantime...while we were walking here. The Meantimes!" he added for emphasis, knowing his friends would be proud of him.

And they were.

"Well done!" and "Bravo!" and "You're a fine fellow!" burst from the group, followed by a happy foot-stomping, high-five-ing, light-dazzling celebration. There was such cheer and noise that Anthony glanced around him, just in case some of the Meantimes had joined them.

The moving bubble of light began a very gentle climb uphill. Their light was not nearly so radiant a contrast to the dark forest now, for the eastern sky was folding itself into the pale pink and the orange of a new day.

CHAPTER 17

Almost Hill

The gentle climb soon ended and for hours they traveled slowly on a narrow, steep path quite crowded by the forest. It was slow going, especially for Mr. Watchit, who was too tall for such a footpath, made by the traffic of small creatures. There was no view beyond the dense barrier of great trees and brambly undergrowth, and even the sun seemed to have trouble finding the ground. Daylight filtered through in an unnatural greenish glow.

"It's like a twisty green tunnel," suggested Anthony. He was remembering that dark passage into the Boulders and wondering how long ago that had happened...and what were his mom and dad doing right now? Were they sitting on the porch, waiting for him? Were they already eating dinner? Or breakfast? Was it already tomorrow? He had lost all track of time. And why were they following this particular path into the forest? Where was Pteros Chronos leading them?

Pteros Chronos seemed hurried. He led them at a brisk pace, whirring up ahead and frequently out of sight because of the twists and turns of the trail. Anthony and Mr. Watchit often turned a corner to find him bobbing on a branch, a spangly orb of light, waiting for them to catch up. He spoke little and never once suggested a rest.

Except for his humming, Mr. Watchit was quiet, too. Anthony loved the sound of Mr. Watchit's humming. It signaled comfort, and Anthony sensed it was Mr. Watchit's way of saying "all is well" without the words. Often Anthony turned around just to watch his new friend, bending and twisting and humming himself through a tight spot, aided by a collapsible walking stick he'd produced from his traveling bag.

Or Anthony would just turn around to watch Mr. Watchit watching things. He was always watching. He would stop and bend or reach, and he didn't hurry the looking. Everything seemed interesting to him—clouds and stones and spider webs and dragonflies. Anthony decided he would tell Mr. Trippett about his new friend who was *observant*, a word Mr. Trippett had taught him, and #37 in his dictionary. Mr. Watchit knew how to pay attention.

At last they came to a stopping place, as quite suddenly the trail twisted sharply and widened into an overlook perched on the very edge of a cliff. It was obviously intended as a place for travelers to rest. Several large, smooth rocks were scattered about. Flat and low to the ground, they were just right for sitting. The view was startling and unexpected.

A strange landscape spread out below and beyond them. The valley seemed planted with row after row of low rounded hills. They were a soft brown color and all identical in size and shape. Behind the hills, rimming the horizon, was a range of sharp-peaked mountains, also identical, hazy with the color of distance.

"But, where is Almost Hill? I mean, which one? Those hills are all alike. That looks like an orchard of hills." Anthony spoke in an anxious sort of voice, due in part to his tired legs and growing hunger. "And look at those mountains!" Here he paused, turning around to find Pteros Chronos, who had remained behind them and very quiet. "Is that an illusion, Mr. Pteros Chronos, sir?"

"No, Anthony. That is no illusion. Those hills are hills. And those mountains are mountains. They are—"

"Here, come here! There's something!" Mr. Watchit was standing dangerously close to the edge of the overlook and pointing straight down. "Excuse the interruption, Pteros Chronos, but right there, Anthony, do you see that? I think that could be Almost Hill."

And it was. Positioned right below them and in front of the first row of the strange brown hills was a small mound. It was just a heap of ground, unremarkable in size and a landmark only for one paying close attention.

"Excellent work, Mr. Watchit!" whispered Pteros Chronos, bursting with multicolored streaks of light, all which spilled out into the airy space above the valley.

"Oh, good for you, Mr. Watchit," said Anthony. "I knew you'd be our best eyes! So that's Almost Hill."

Anthony was looking through the binoculars now and could see how the trail divided at the base of the mound and then continued in two different directions. Here was the choice he was expected to make, and his eyes followed the faint outline of each path. One led east while the other angling to the northwest, just as Pteros Chronos had said.

Pteros Chronos had remained apart, allowing Anthony and Mr. Watchit enough time to discover the steep trail that would lead them down into the valley and right to Almost Hill.

Gathered back together, Mr. Watchit suggested they have celebrative tea. "In honor of our discovery and our stomachs," he said with a chuckle. In no time at all they were seated around a small fire with ginger tea brewing in the blue enamel teapot. Mr. Watchit produced two carefully wrapped packages from his brown bag—apricot scones and tiny meat and potato pies. Anthony asked for seconds and thirds, and then he asked for the recipes.

"So my mother can make them at home." His eyes were large with the thought.

Mr. Watchit recited the ingredients the best he could and Anthony did all he could to remember the list, but his brain was full of many things and, most likely, there would be omissions and substitutions of ingredients by the time he told his mother. The apricot scones and the meat and potato pies would never taste as they did on that overlook with Mr. Watchit and Pteros Chronos.

"I could only lead you to the overlook," Pteros Chronos explained as they finished their tea. "As Time Flies, we are under obligation and oath not to reveal the location of Almost Hill. Thus protected, this site and its story remain only for those who come with a vision. That would be you, Mr. Watchit, and you, too, Anthony." He paused for a moment, finishing a very tiny bite of scone before continuing. "Now you have found the site, and I must tell you the story. Please arrange yourselves comfortably. It is a long story."

CHAPTER 18

All Mole Hills

Pteros Chronos settled on a rock near Anthony and Mr. Watchit. He had stopped whirring, having folded his iridescent wings within his radiant light. Anthony wondered often about Pteros Chronos. What was he, really? Was he something solid and hot to the touch, or would he behave like a vapor and disappear through Anthony's fingers? When Pteros Chronos encircled him with light, Anthony felt such warmth and confidence. What did he do? And what did he do when he wasn't being a guide? Did he have a family? Were there little Time Fly children? Did they go to school? Did they finish all their schoolwork? Were some Time Flies still hanging like bats from the ceiling inside the Boulders, waiting for assignments? Now was not the time to ask those questions. Pteros Chronos had cleared his throat, a signal Anthony did understand. It was time for a story.

"From Time *Immemorial* ... that means, Anthony, from a time as far back as anyone can remember, this valley has been the home of generation upon generation of moles." Pteros Chronos began in a voice he saved just for storytelling. It was deep and clear, and every word was spoken with importance. Anthony was hypnotized from the first sentence.

"Up until a few decades ago," he continued, "all of what you see there," he spotlighted the valley below them, "was called All Mole Hills. It was a lovely valley back then, dotted with hundreds of small irregular heaps of earth, similar to the one you spotted below us. I still remember flying with my father above this valley when I was but a young Time Fly. My father explained the hills to me and told me about the shy creatures who lived in burrows underground." Pteros Chronos sighed with the memory. "That was such a pleasant excursion, one of my first long-distance trips.

"It seems this valley has always been a perfect place for moles. The climate is mild, the earth is soft and loamy, just the right texture and composition for digging their amazing labyrinth of corridors. Hmm ... *labyrinth.* Anthony, I am certain you know that word from the story of Theseus and the Minotaur."

Anthony nodded in an exaggerated way, remembering the time he made a labyrinth of boxes in his backyard and pretended to be Theseus. He had been armed with a cardboard sword and a ball of yarn from his mother's knitting basket.

"Yes? I thought so. We will return to Theseus later. Now, back to the Moles. Earthworms were plentiful, and the moles' underground larders were always full.

"A *larder?*" Anthony had raised his hand and his eyebrows with the question.

"Oh, yes. A larder is like a pantry, Anthony. It is a place to store food. A lovely word. Lovely place too," glowed the Time Fly.

"So, you see, the moles had saved plenty of food. Their enemies were few. Baby moles thrived. The population grew. For so many years the moles lived here in peace and harmony, even, I am told, often seen above ground in those early days.

"But, as time passed, more and more outsiders traveled through the valley. Some began to speak of 'land potential' and 'real estate,' ideas I fail to understand. Little by little these outsiders pressured one mole family after another into selling their hills and moving to Elsewhere. The outsiders, you see, had plans to build mountains. Apparently they wanted a higher view, high enough to see the River Endless or even as far away as Elsewhere. What you see in that line of mountains, and these closer hills..." and here Pteros Chronos paused, giving Anthony and Mr. Watchit time to look again at the identical mountains and identical hills, "...well, those were all once molehills, homes to families of moles, just wanting to live their lives in peace. The mountains you see...those were the first molehills sold. And all of those smaller hills out there? They are on their way to becoming mountains. Those in charge believe controls should be exerted to keep a sameness to this growth, so that no mountain would diminish the value of the others."

Again Pteros Chronos paused, sensing his audience needed time to absorb this part of the story. "Only one sturdy family of moles has remained. That is the reason we call this place "Almost Hill." It is our code name, an effort to protect this last mole family and this one last molehill."

Anthony and Mr. Watchit looked again at the field of identical hills and then down at the lone molehill in the valley right below them. Anthony finally spoke. "But, Pteros Chronos, sir, that is a terrible story. What's to become of the moles?"

"The moles continue to do what they do best, burrowing through the earth, raising their young, and keeping an ear to the ground. That is why we needed to come this way, Anthony. Nothing passes through this valley without the moles' knowledge. Like the ancient people, they hear the deep vibrations. They stay in touch with whatever touches the earth. They could have information about your airplane."

Anthony's eyes had widened in disbelief. He was feeling an ache in his heart. Something was horribly wrong. "It's good that they may know something about my airplane, sir, but...what about the moles? What can we do to help the moles?"

"Well, Anthony, perhaps another time you can be of help to them. (That other time did come for Anthony, but that is another story.) But now, it is actually they who may be of help to you. We must proceed downhill quickly. Where the trail divides, we are most likely to receive information or clues. By the way, Anthony, that word 'clue' comes from an ancient Greek word for a ball of string or yarn. So, you see, we have returned to Theseus. Do you remember how he used yarn as a clue to find his way back through the labyrinth?"

"Ahh," grinned Mr. Watchit. "The strength of a yarn indeed!"

Pteros Chronos and Mr. Watchit chuckled quietly, though Anthony was unaware of any joke. He was still thinking of the moles being forced to leave their homes.

"And now, let me warn you." Pteros Chronos shifted quickly to his serious voice. "Do not expect to see any moles. They are secretive and highly skilled in under-cover work. They have creative ways of sending messages. If they do have information, it will likely come disguised. You will need to be very alert, Anthony.

Mr. Watchit, you, sir, must be prepared to assist Anthony. He may need your help. Now. Let us be off, eyes and ears at the ready."

Sensing an urgency in these directions, Anthony and Mr. Watchit carefully extinguished the fire, repacked and zipped the traveling bag, and followed Pteros Chronos down the steep descent into the valley. Here the path turned a sharp right and wound back along the base of the hill to that spot they had seen from the overlook, the spot where the trail divided around a small, unremarkable heap of ground.

For a long time Anthony and Mr. Watchit waited silently, right in front of Almost Hill, hoping directions would come quickly and out loud. They scanned the area with the binoculars and inspected all around for hidden information. They felt the ground for vibrations. They studied the clouds and listened to the wind. The sun traveled across the sky, and long shadows darkened patterns on the ground.

At one point Mr. Watchit and Anthony realized that Pteros Chronos had disappeared.

"No reason for alarm," Mr. Watchit spoke quietly, handing Anthony the tin of crackers and the thermos of water. "I would suppose he enjoys a bit of wandering from time to time."

"I know. Besides, I am the one who must decide which way to go," Anthony whispered, not wanting to scare away any moles.

Finally Pteros Chronos returned from what he called a *surveillance* mission, though he offered no information, and he did not seem surprised that they had received no direction from the moles.

"Moles are not easily hurried," was all he said, after he explained the word surveillance to Anthony. "A lovely word, Anthony. Related to *survey*. You may want to add those words to your dictionary."

Mr. Watchit, relieved by the Time Fly's return, stretched out on his back, covered his face with his safari hat, and announced a nap.

Anthony, curious about a flutter of small gray birds, had walked closer to a cluster of brambly bushes. Taking Mr. Watchit's binoculars, he leaned against a tree to watch.

The birds were nest-building, an amazing thing to see up close. Two tiny birds brought twigs and bits of leaves, the fluff from dandelions, and even a strand of blue string. They were weaving and tucking these materials together...with string...string. What was it about string?

Anthony suddenly looked back at his companions. Both were dozing. But shouldn't he wake them? Wasn't string a clue?

"String! String! That's it!" Anthony shouted. "Here's the clue, Pteros Chronos, a piece of string!"

Pteros Chronos quickly awoke and whirred over to Anthony. He beamed directly on the small twiggy nest, now empty of birds, but threaded with bright blue string. "String!" he whispered.

"String, you say? What's this about string?" Mr. Watchit was jolted from a dream about racecars. He fumbled about for his safari hat, wondering why he was driving in a race without a proper helmet. And why were Anthony and Pteros Chronos occupied with something in the bushes when his race was about to begin? Then he remembered. "A clue you say?" Mr. Watchit said, smiling as he walked toward his friends. Though for just a flash of time he remained somewhat poised for the pistol shot that would start the race.

"It's just like the story of Theseus. String! Look, Mr. Watchit!" Anthony was so excited it was hard for him to be quiet. "We need to take this path, this one on the right, leading east. Oh, thank you, little birds! Thank you! And, moles, wherever you are, thank you, too!"

Pteros Chronos and Mr. Watchit cheered for Anthony in a quiet sort of way, aware of the noise their excitement had caused. They didn't want to disturb the moles. (Besides, they were eager to continue their journey.)

While Pteros Chronos beamed toward the path leading east, signaling his readiness for departure, Anthony walked back to Almost Hill. "Good-bye, good Moles," he whispered. "Thank you. I hope I get to really see you some day."

Meanwhile, Mr. Watchit, whose racecar dream had drifted far away by now, marked the very rare grey-throated bush nesters in his bird book.

"Good-bye, good birds," he whispered and, mindful of the need for secrecy, wrote only the initials *A. H.* and the word *string.*

CHAPTER 19

The River Endless

If Pteros Chronos or Mr. Watchit ever doubted the importance of that piece of blue string, they never mentioned it. From the moment of Anthony's discovery, they were buoyed by his bird nest find, and all three were swept along by a current of optimism leading them eastward and closer to finding the airplane. This trail was far different from the rugged climb they experienced in the morning. Broad and easy going, it looped in and out of shadow-slanted clearings that edged the forest. It was just the sort of pathway that fostered good feelings and a gladness to be outside.

Even Pteros Chronos, usually so serious about their journey, seemed jubilant with shimmering energy. He zoomed and careened along the trail, turning fancy patterns and entertaining his companions with a light show much like fireworks on the Fourth of July. Traveling with Anthony and Mr. Watchit had given him a new perspective. For though he knew these lands, and all the pathways, the flows of forgotten creeks, the sinkings of swamps, the silences of the secret places and the folk who lived here, this knowledge was from a distance above and not in the company of friends. He beamed with the joy of a shared adventure and often allowed Anthony to bound ahead and lead them.

They had traveled several hours when they neared a noisy stream, and Mr. Watchit suggested they stop for tea. It was a grand place to rest their legs and wings and listen to the sounds of water, which was also on a journey. Anthony spread out the yellow tablecloth and watched Mr. Watchit unpack egg-salad sandwiches, apple slices, and a small strawberry-iced raisin cake. Egg salad. Anthony tried not to think too much about it, as eggs of any sort caused him to gag, and he didn't want to appear rude or picky. He busied himself with the burner contraption, helped Mr. Watchit light a small fire, and readied the raspberry tea, all the while remembering stories of prisoners who ate cockroaches and lizards, and wondering if egg salad tasted similar.

It was that lazy time of late afternoon when the day is beginning to fold up and the evening is preparing to spread out. The travelers were quiet, enjoying the light, the splashing of the stream, and a memorable feast. By the time Anthony had eaten three slices of raisin cake, he was just "too full" to try an egg-salad sandwich. He apologized, and was silently grateful that the rule of saving dessert for last was apparently unknown to Mr. Watchit or Pteros Chronos.

Even after their meal, they stayed, just listening to the sounds of this place, knit together by the invisible threads of their growing friendship. Though Anthony felt safe and protected and certainly hopeful about finding his airplane, he wondered silently about where they would spend the night. He thought about how good it would be to crawl into his own bed and pull up Granny Ellis's quilt all snug around him. He wondered if Polaris might be looking through the window for him. He wondered what his mom would fix for supper tonight (pizza maybe?) and if Mr. Watchit had little packets of pizza in his traveling bag. And then again, where they would be when night came?

"Where does this path lead us, Mr. Pteros Chronos, sir?" Anthony's question stepped right out into their quiet circle.

"Lead us? Well, I suppose any path can 'lead us' to any number of places. It depends on where you choose to stop. You decide that, Anthony. And, if you choose to leave the path and seek your own route, then you create yet a new path, one that allows you to travel...until you stop. The stopping place is your choice. Yes, indeed, the traveler decides where a path leads." Pteros Chronos shimmered as he spoke. Deep thinking always made him glow with greater brilliance. "But," Pteros Chronos suddenly seemed to remember something, and his words reflected hurry. "Shall we move along? There is something I would like to show you while we still have daylight."

So they packed up the brown traveling bag and headed down the path with the Time Fly leading them. There was no other conversation until a faint breeze caught Anthony's attention.

"Hamburgers!" he said aloud. "I smell hamburgers!" The group stopped and all took deep breaths. Mr. Watchit's eyes squinted for recognition though he, like Pteros Chronos, was unfamiliar with the term *hamburgers*. "Do you think someone might be cooking hamburgers?" Anthony gazed in the direction of the smell. East.

"Possibly an early blooming Yanible tree," suggested Pteros Chronos. "Often it imitates the aroma of outdoor cooking. I've been fooled many times."

"Does this ... this Yanible tree taste like hamburgers?" Anthony was envisioning a tree, an orchard even, with hamburgers blooming like flowers.

"Well, I do not know that taste, Anthony, though I believe it to be a sort of sandwich."

"Yes! It's a meat sandwich, with lettuce and tomatoes, and sometimes onions, but I never order onions, and maybe ketchup. I always add cheese. But it's nothing like an egg-salad sandwich..." and then careful not to hurt feelings, he continued, "It isn't made with eggs at all!"

Anthony glanced at Mr. Watchit, just to make sure. He didn't know if Mr. Watchit was sensitive about the food he so generously shared.

But Mr. Watchit had moved on. He had sighted birds in the trees ahead and was rapidly turning pages in his book to identify them.

"Strange indeed," he said. "A third kind of waterfowl. There! Right over there in the trees." He pointed with his long nose. His hands were busy noting the presence of the web-footed, blue-crested High-Waders. "There must be more water around than we have seen."

He was exactly right. For as they rounded the next bend, a river appeared, wide and slow-moving and silver in the fading light. This was what Pteros Chronos had wanted them to see, and it was a grand sight indeed.

The path ended in a muddy bank. A rickety boat dock nosed itself out into the current. Circling a single post at the end of the dock was a thick rope attached to a small wooden boat painted white and blue. A sign on the post read:

Ferry Service
Please Ring Bell
Ratty

There was no bell that Anthony could see. And who was this Ratty?

"This is the River Endless," said Pteros Chronos, sweeping a beam of light across the muddy bank and reflecting off the silver water. "As a river, it flows to the sea, and then as cloud, it flows over the earth, and then again it flows as rain, back to earth. A cycle of endless gifts, ancient and protected," he paused as if just the sighting of the River Endless were a solemn event.

Anthony and Mr. Watchit stood quite still, breathing in the river smells and sensing great importance in this quietly whishing, deep-traveling water. "This will be our stopping place for tonight," Pteros Chronos spoke directly to Anthony. "Tomorrow, Anthony, you will decide whether we cross the river or continue our journey on this side."

He had just finished speaking when a large creature, easily Anthony's size, stepped through the bushes and into the clearing. He wore frayed blue shorts and a faded t-shirt. A dirty white nautical cap sat at an angle on his head. He had friendly bright eyes, long whiskers, and a tail, and in one paw he carried what must be the bell mentioned on the sign.

Anthony blinked. This must be Ratty, for he was, indeed, a rat.

CHAPTER 20

Ratty

"Ahh, Pteros Chronos! My friend! Splendid to see you!" The rat stretched out his arms in a grand gesture of welcome, ringing the ferry bell *unintentionally,* though that sound added to a spirit of hospitality and good cheer. "It's been quite a long spell. Let's have a good chat, shall we? Catching ourselves up to one another."

"Indeed, Ratty. Much too long!" said Pteros Chronos, expanding and encircling the rat in luminous brilliance. "Let me introduce my friends, Anthony and Mr. Exactus Watchit," he said, resuming his normal size, but still bobbing with flashes of visible joy.

"Please call me Ratty. All my friends do," said the rat, removing his hat, bowing low and extending a paw, first to Mr. Watchit and then to Anthony. "But before we visit, I must return this bell to the post out there on the dock." He walked quickly out to the end of the dock, deposited the bell on the post, brushed his small paws together several times to indicate a job completed, and then rejoined his visitors. "I keep misplacing it…found it in the garden this time. Won't do a'tall, busy as I am. Lots are here for the Gathering, Pteros Chronos. A very big gathering. Lots of business for the ferry. Now then. Let me see…" he smiled warmly and patted Anthony on the shoulder. "Are you the small boy of the airplane? The Anthony?"

"Yes, sir, I am," Anthony's eyes were wide with the wonder of this talking rat who knew his name. "But how did you know that…Mr. Ratty?"

"Well, the Moles, bless them. They send signals, you know. Nothing goes on without their knowing of it. We thought you might be coming our way. And, yes, there has been talk of your airplane. Up and down the river."

"Talk!" Anthony and Mr. Watchit spoke the word at the same time.

"Yes, talk. Rumors perhaps. Nothing definite, but definitely talk. The latest news came from Alice and that rabbit…I can never remember that rabbit's name. They arrived just this morning, from the north, I believe—though it could have been the south." Ratty cocked his head and shifted his view to somewhere in the sky, as if that might be a place for answers about Alice and the rabbit.

"Have they seen my airplane?" Anthony's eyes remained wide, hopeful.

"Well, I'm not one to spread rumors," Ratty smiled back at Anthony. "You'll have to ask Alice. She has lots of stories to share. Some of them may concern your airplane."

With that Ratty turned to Pteros Chronos and the two of them fell right into the easy sort of conversation that marks old friendships, regardless of time apart.

It was a good time for Anthony and Mr. Watchit to wander over to the river, for there was much to see, even in the fading light.

"Good news, Anthony," said Mr. Watchit quietly as they approached the boat dock. "About your airplane. It seems we are on the right path. Perhaps tomorrow we will find it. But look! Look at this river! Magnificent!" Mr. Watchit whispered magnificent to himself, as if he sensed a kind of magic flowing before him, and he did not want to break a spell. He carefully placed his traveling bag on a grassy patch near the bank and stepped awkwardly upon the boat dock. "Do you suppose this is safe, Anthony? I've never stepped on such a structure. In truth, I've never even seen a river before, except in travel catalogues and on maps. Oh, Anthony. I think I shall learn to swim. And fish. And boat around. Oh my! What a spectacle! What a thing to see!"

But to Anthony's thinking it was Mr. Watchit who was the thing to see. His long arms and long legs bent in awkward angles as he jerked and lunged his way down the boat dock. There were no railings and the dock swayed under his weight, but somehow Mr. Watchit managed to reach the post at the end. Anthony hoped Mr. Watchit would be careful not to knock the bell off its perch and into the river swirling below him.

While Mr. Watchit stood, breathing deeply of the wondrous scene around him, Anthony studied the far bank for any sign of the Alice Ratty had mentioned.

He saw a small dock, likely the other half of Ratty's ferry service, but the darkness was smudging all the features across the river, and he detected no movement. And there was that smell again. The Yanible tree. Anthony wished for light enough to see those trees. Just at that moment, as if wishing made it so, he did see light, several winking lights, scattered up and down across the river.

"Campfires! Look, Mr. Watchit. Over there. Campfires! Somebody's camping over there!"

But Ratty's voice sounded from behind them.

"Come along, Anthony and Watchit. Come. Follow me. Too dark to cross tonight. I never ferry after Sundown. Spend the night with me. Plenty of room. And I have a splendid stew, made just today and good bread. More than enough for company. Please come." With that Ratty disappeared beyond the bushes, though his voice trailed behind. "And watch your head, Watchit. You may have to fold over a bit."

Pteros Chronos waited for them, shining light on the path. It led them through a hedge of thick bushes and upriver along the muddy bank to a great willow tree decorated with festive lights, looking more like an outdoor restaurant than the home of a river rat. Various outdoor chairs and tables surrounded a lively campfire. Anthony smelled something delicious coming from a great iron kettle hanging above the fire.

CHAPTER 21

Kumquats and Giants

B acon. Frying bacon. Dishes clacking together. Breakfast. Time to get up for school. His mother would soon call him from downstairs.

"Hurry, Anthony!" she would say.

He stretched and sat up, realizing he was tangled in a cocoon of quilts, under the arms of that big willow tree, and it was Ratty who was frying bacon over the campfire. Anthony wasn't home. Not yet.

He began to put the pieces of last night back together. This Ratty fellow, who seemed somehow familiar to Anthony. Someone named Alice who had news of the airplane. Ratty's house here on the riverbank. Too late to cross. Something about kumquats...and giants? Had they spoken of giants last night or had he dreamed that?

It had been so dark when they arrived, he had not seen much of Ratty's house, though he did remember this big willow tree and the threading of electric lights like a tiny constellation in the branches above him. And that delicious stew, and being so tired, and Ratty getting all these quilts for him and Mr. Watchit. And Mr. Watchit saying something about "sleeping under the stars."

Where was Mr. Watchit? And Pteros Chronos?

He looked around, now seeing an open doorway to Ratty's home under the tree roots. A stone walk led to the door, which was fashioned from a packing crate, still faintly advertising Simon's Green Beans. A fenced garden off to the side guarded several rows of tiny green shoots, and watered, most likely, by a bucket apparatus strung on a line that linked garden to river. Several fruit trees bloomed beyond the garden, and spilling from an open tool shed were more buckets and shovels, a ladder, and a collection of bits and pieces of tools Anthony couldn't identify. A canoe rested belly-up on sawhorses, and scattered around the fire pit where Ratty busied with breakfast were those unmatched chairs and tables he had noticed last night. It was a home of industry and hospitality, and all of it under the arms of the huge willow, with a clear view to the river.

"Good morning, Anthony." Ratty had noticed Anthony sitting up, still wrapped in quilts. "Though you're looking more like a hungry caterpillar, all wrapped up in a cocoon."

Anthony yawned, "Good Morning, Mr. Ratty."

"It's a fine morning." Ratty turned back to the iron skillet. "A great day ahead for us!"

"Yes, Mr. Ratty, a great day." Anthony yawned some more. He noticed the grayness of the sky and the river it mirrored, and he wondered if this was the sort of weather that Ratty enjoyed. He wondered again where Mr. Watchit and Pteros Chronos were.

"Come. Sit over here, Anthony. Have a cup of tea. Then you and I will share an omelet. Watchit and Pteros Chronos have gone fishing, up river. They'll not be long. Too windy for fishing today."

Breakfast was delicious. And there is just nothing like a lovely cup of tea and a good omelet around a warming campfire to encourage conversation.

"Mr. Ratty, sir," Anthony was still trying to remember the events of last night. "I'm wondering about something. Last night. I think you were telling Mr. Watchit about campfires across the river. And I think you were talking about kumquats and giants. But I can't remember what you said. I think that's when I fell asleep."

"Kumquats!" Ratty laughed. "I think you mean OUATs?"

"OUATs? OUATs! Yes, that's the word! What are OUATs?"

"Well, the OUATs are the reason there were campfires across the river last night. It's our big Gathering. We get together several times a year, though there are always OUATs somewhere, gathered together and telling stories. That's what we do, don't you see. Stories, that's the thing."

"Stories...so do you mean people telling stories?" Anthony squinted his eyes together in an effort to understand. "OUATs are people?"

More laughter from Ratty.

"Yes and no. Characters. We are characters, Anthony. Each letter in OUATs stands for a word. An *acronym*, I believe it is called. We are the Once Upon A Times. That "s" at the end just means there is more than just one of us. OUATs. We are a gathering of story characters. And we are not content to have lived just once upon a time within a book, I might add. We are charged with the responsibility of keeping the stories alive. And so we tell our stories, and retell them. A high calling and a wonderful responsibility. I believe you will recognize many of us."

Anthony was quiet. He was sorting this new information and all of these clues. He had thought Ratty was familiar. Now he felt sure of it.

"Mr. Ratty, sir," Anthony's voice dropped to a whisper, just in case he had uncovered a secret. "Are you maybe THE Ratty I have read about? Just like I am

THE Anthony you heard about? Do you have a friend named Toad?"

"Yes, indeed." Ratty laughed loudly. "Toad and Mole and Badger. Yes, that's precisely who I am. Good for you, Anthony. So you have read our story. I am not surprised."

"The Wind in the Willows!" Anthony exclaimed. "My father read me your story. We have our very own book. Well, it's my father's book. He has had it since he was a little boy. Oh, wow! I can't wait to tell him! I have met the real Ratty!" Ratty busied himself with the campfire and offered no comment. Too much attention obviously made him uncomfortable.

"And the giants? Were you really talking about giants last night? Are there really giants over there?" Anthony looked hard at the smudgy grey landscape across the river.

"Well, of course. Though they are mostly a jolly sort. Years ago we had to insist on good behavior. There was an unfortunate incident, which we won't discuss. The giants had to sign a pledge. Now we just have to watch them when they move about. They are not so careful where they sit, and they do eat a lot. They are much like the bears, though not so hairy. And they never rise before noon. But they are good folk, and they do love a story."

"Oh, Mr. Ratty. I am so happy. I love stories, too. Is the Alice you told me about... the one with news of the airplane...is she perhaps the Alice from the Looking Glass and Wonderland? And that rabbit...that's the white rabbit. I know that story!" Anthony's eyes stared into some distant place as he began to think of all the story characters who might be right across the river.

"Yes, Alice and the white rabbit. And let me see...there are so many. Three of the Narnia children arrived yesterday, though not Edmund, at least, not yet. Rumpelstiltskin is here, and Robin Hood. A boy named Tom, and Nancy Drew, and Dorothy and Toto, though Toto missed our last gathering because of a bicycle accident. Several giants and the Pied Piper—he brought quite a following. Oh, yes. King Arthur and Frodo...do you know him? A hobbit, he is. Oh, there are so many others. Many, I must confess I do not know personally. But you will see them all, and I am quite certain you will learn something about your airplane."

It was just almost too amazing for Anthony to believe. Story characters, alive and gathering together and telling stories, and right across the Endless. And news of his airplane, just right across that river. For one tiny bit of a moment, the thought of finding his airplane collided with the thought of returning home and leaving this adventure behind. It was a flash of a collision only, for he was eager to meet the OUATs.

"When can we cross, Mr. Ratty, sir?"

"Well, there's no rush. The Gathering goes on for days, for weeks. We'll tidy up. I always take a morning walk, check the garden for snails. I need to fill the bird feeders and start my bread. Perhaps I'll finish patching that canoe. I'd say we'll be ready around half past noon, if the weather stays this pleasant. Lovely gray sky and, did you notice? The wind has picked up."

Anthony looked up. He smelled rain and, sure enough, the wind was moving through the willow tree.

CHAPTER 22

First Crossing

When they gathered back at the boat dock, the gray morning had lengthened into a gray afternoon. Gusty winds whipped at the trees and bothered the river, and splinters of rain pricked Anthony's face. The opposite bank was just a darker smudge of gray, the boat dock barely visible. Except for Mr. Watchit's yellow rain slicker, everything seemed drained of color, as if all the greens and blues of yesterday had been blown downstream.

Anthony had spent the morning watching the opposite bank for any sign of the OUATs. While Ratty had busied about planting radishes and mending a leak in the upturned canoe, and Pteros Chronos and Mr. Watchit had gone fishing again, he had watched. And even though he saw nothing but swirls and drifts of fog, and he was soaked with drizzle, he continued to watch, until they had assembled for Ratty's instructions.

The weather made Anthony uneasy. Throughout the morning he had sensed this was not a good day to cross the river in Ratty's small boat. Though he did not speak it, he knew his father would never allow such a trip, even to see story characters who called themselves the Once Upon A Times. A terrible wave of homesickness swept over him. He felt queasy, and he wished he were home again. He wondered if Ratty ever canceled a ferry trip.

Yet it was clear that they were crossing. Pteros Chronos and Mr. Watchit seemed eager, and Ratty appeared unaware of the weather. He was a river rat, after all, and happiest in or on the water. Now he was Captain Ratty, wearing an old white jacket with brass buttons and military braid, his Navy cap sitting lopsided on his head. He gave directions clearly and with authority.

"The boat cannot carry but two of us at a time. I'll take you first, Anthony. Pteros Chronos and Watchit, you wait here. Won't take long."

Anthony squinted and looked up. There was no sign the rain would stop. He glanced at Mr. Watchit standing right beside him, almost at attention. Underneath the yellow hood, his blue eyes, quick and alert, were fastened to Ratty and his instructions.

Raindrops rolled off his long nose though he did not seem to notice. The bulky presence of his traveling bag under the rain slicker ballooned his shape, and Anthony suddenly imagined him bobbing down the Endless like an inflated water toy. But Mr. Watchit couldn't swim. Anthony looked at him again. Mr. Watchit couldn't swim, yet here he was, standing in the rain, eager to cross this river, all because of Anthony's airplane.

Pteros Chronos bobbed about as a fuzzy light in the rain while Ratty talked on and on about the direction of the wind and the general drift of currents, and used words like *port* and *starboard* to explain positions on the boat. Pteros Chronos did not like delays or long speeches, and Anthony recognized his friend's impatience. But just seeing him was a comfort. This effort for him, so that he could find his airplane and get back home. And there was that feeling again—a tug at his stomach, or was it his heart?

"I will signal when we reach the opposite dock." Ratty spoke over his shoulder as he jumped into the boat, splashing a pool of water that had collected in the bottom. He lifted the small seat in the stern and held up a square flashlight and an orange life jacket. "Dot, dot, dot. Three quick flashes means 'All's well.' Morse code, you know. Well, my version of Morse code. Then I'll want you, Pteros Chronos to buzz right across. You are to keep Anthony company while I return for Watchit," Ratty paused briefly, looking in turn at his three companions. "All set?"

Anthony nodded.

Pteros Chronos flashed back, 'dot, dot, dot.'

"Yes, sir. Aye, aye, sir. Thank you, Mr. Ratty, Captain, sir," Mr. Watchit had raised a yellow arm in salute. "We will await your return, sir. Here's a hand, Anthony. I believe this is when one might say 'Bon Voyage.'"

Even with Mr. Watchit's help, Anthony's jump was stiff, and he landed off center, again splashing the collecting water and causing the little boat to wobble back and forth, very close to dipping right into the river.

"Easy. Easy, Anthony." Ratty motioned to the stern seat and handed him the life jacket.

"Now, toss us the line, Watchit. And we're off!"

And they were off and quickly too. The small boat, released from its tether was impatient for the swift water, and Ratty, with a fancy flourish of the oars, lost little time rowing them skillfully into that wide sweep of the Endless where he positioned the craft, straight and true toward the opposite dock.

He smiled broadly at Anthony, who was hunched over, his face mostly hidden under a jacket hood, dark with moisture, his small hands gripping the sides of the craft.

"Nothing to fret about, Anthony. We'll soon be on the other side, and you'll be visiting with the OUATs." He raised his voice over the rain and the wind and the splatting of waves that hit them broadside and splashed into the boat. "Nothing to fret about," he repeated louder. "You're traveling on the Endless, magical among all waters, these are. Any sort of dip into this river...well, no harm will come to you, Anthony." He paused for a moment, looking backward to check his direction. "Look around you. There's so much to see. Ahhh...What a beautiful world. This, right here. This beautiful river."

Anthony lifted his head. He smiled weakly at Ratty and looked around, knowing it was the polite thing to do. Everything was gray—the rainy sky above them, the rushing and churning waters around them, the gloomy land hemming the river. Gray and wet. And cold. Their tiny boat was just a speck in all of this gray. How could Ratty find beauty in any of this?

Anthony shivered. He turned back just to see how far they had traveled. Just to make sure Pteros Chronos and Mr. Watchit had not disappeared into the fog.

There they were! A pale scrap of yellow and a dim beam of light still on the shore. And here was Ratty. Anthony looked back and forth, connecting these dots and realizing he was the middle dot. He was surrounded by grayness, but bound together with friends who cared for him.

And, just at that moment—just as Anthony smiled a real smile at Ratty, a smile that said, "Thank you!"

and "You are right about the beauty of this world!"—just at that very moment, he sensed a brightness behind him.

A brilliant stream of sparkling light was stretching itself across the Endless and coming toward their boat. Like another river flowing on top of the Endless, it seemed to gather up all the hidden sunlight and starlight and moonlight and transform the air and the water into a flood of swirling radiance. Anthony looked back at Ratty. His whiskered face reflected the oncoming light though he continued to row steadily, as though nothing extraordinary were happening.

As the light spun and looped nearer, Anthony saw millions of tiny specks, iridescent bubbles, or maybe diamonds or star crystals. Just before this brilliance overwhelmed the boat and its two occupants, the light submerged, illuminating the deep blue green of an underwater world below, and then resurfaced, surrounding them in a foamy, glittering spray that lifted the boat and bore it quickly to the dock. And then the light vanished.

Ratty secured the boat and helped Anthony step across to the dock. He signaled to Pteros Chronos, who responded with "dot, dot, dot." Then he waited with Anthony until the Time Fly had meteored across the river and hovered breathless on the dock. Ratty never mentioned the light.

"Wow! Mr. Pteros Chronos! You're back! In no time!" Anthony smiled at his friend, a master of illusions.

"Well, not exactly, Anthony." He was breathing hard. "I believe that particular passage was exactly one minute and thirty-seven seconds to be exact."

***

In another effort at exactness, it is worth noting that years later when Anthony described this event to his father, he used the word *tsunami* to describe that flood of light, causing his father to raise his eyebrows slightly and open the dictionary to the *T*s.

"Was it possibly more like a *deluge* or a *surge*?" his father asked, looking up both of those words, too.

Anthony shook his head. "No, it was a small, helpful tsunami."

Like all things magical, this river of light remained a difficult experience to explain, without exaggeration.

CHAPTER 23
Second Crossing

It was clear from the start that Mr. Watchit was just too big for Ratty's boat. He folded himself up to fit, but his knees came up to his chin, and he looked more like a yellow folding chair wearing a life preserver than a passenger. As the pool of water in the bottom of the boat had grown larger, Mr. Watchit carefully placed his traveling bag between his knees and atop his feet. The bag and his weight submerged the tiny boat to within inches of the river. It began raining harder, and the current was stronger. With such rain and wind, it was difficult for Ratty and Mr. Watchit to hear one another.

But Ratty was a superb oarsman, and the little boat, though struggling with the weather and the extra weight, made progress. The crossing, in fact, was almost without incident. Ratty yelled over the noise of the river and the rain, telling Mr. Watchit about the beaver community up the river and the trading post run by magpies down river, around the bend. Mr. Watchit yelled back, asking about the Sheers, a series of dangerous cliffs he had once seen on an old map. But there was no time to talk about the Sheers. Ratty was concentrating on his approach to the boat dock. That was when Mr. Watchit suddenly stood up, readying himself to step onto the dock. Things went badly wrong.

For, standing up, by someone unskilled in the balancing needs of a boat, especially in weather such as it was, creates a flood of problems. When he stood and hoisted his traveling bag over his shoulder, Mr. Watchit overloaded that left (or port) side. At the same time the boat was tipping, a gust of wind caught the nose of the craft and, despite Ratty's best efforts, spun it around into the strong current headed quickly downstream. Ratty, calling for Mr. Watchit to sit down, simply yelled, "Watchit! Watchit!" and Mr. Watchit, not accustomed yet to this abbreviation of his name by Ratty and thinking something needed watching, suddenly jerked around to the right (or starboard), dropping his traveling bag down with a splash. That motion tipped the boat and its occupants far enough to the right that the Endless poured right into the craft, sweeping Mr. Watchit's traveling bag out and into the great beyond of the swiftly traveling river.

All of this had taken but a moment. Later Mr. Watchit would explain what caused his confusion, but in that moment nothing was clear except that his brown traveling bag had become a boat.

Anthony watched with horror as Mr. Watchit lurched to grab the bag. The river was too quick, though, and the bag, broad and apparently waterproof, easily escaped into the frothy current. No amount of fast swimming, even by a river rat, would have caught up with that sturdy vessel, its handles standing upright like short sails, its mysterious contents headed for some unknown destination downriver.

It was Ratty's skill once again which prevented Mr. Watchit from becoming a man overboard. Knowing his responsibility lay with his passenger and his boat, he turned the craft around and muscled a now quite submerged boat against the current and finally back to the dock.

No one had spoken. It was not until Mr. Watchit stepped, dripping upon the dock that Anthony gasped a breath and began to sob.

"Oh, Mr. Watchit! I'm so sorry! I am so sorry, Mr. Watchit. Your traveling bag! Oh, Mr. Watchit, are you all right?"

And though these words are now easily readable on this page, what Anthony blubbered was hardly understandable, a frequent problem when sobs and wailings overpower words. What was understandable was his relief that Mr. Watchit was safe. Anthony's concern for the loss of the traveling bag was certainly a part of his distress, but he was old enough to know how close they had come to a real loss.

Ratty continued to make fast the boat and bail out what he could with a bucket he kept for such emergencies. Later he would express his sympathy for Mr. Watchit's lost bag and a cheerful offer to teach him "a bit about boating." Pteros Chronos had immediately enlarged into a warming brightness, surrounding Mr. Watchit and Anthony, Ratty and the boat. Beyond the lifting of their spirits, they began to dry out.

"Ratty said the Endless is magical, Mr. Watchit, and that no harm will come if you take a dip in it. I think that means your bag too, Mr. Watchit. It will be okay, too." Anthony had mostly stopped crying, but his eyes glistened with tears.

"Well, certainly it will," replied Mr. Watchit. He bent down to Anthony's level, eye to eye, and spoke gently to him. "It was a wonderful bag, though I didn't use it for traveling until now. It belonged to my grandfather, Edward Watchit. He was quite a traveler. A good storyteller, too. Yes, I will miss its feel in my hands. And that blue teapot. I hope someone will find use for it. Came from my grandmother, it did."

He paused, still bent and close to Anthony. He placed a steady hand on Anthony's shoulder. "But, Anthony, I am lighter now. Lighter. All of these pockets

I kept so full of watches. I thought they were time keepers, but they were really keeping me... I was weighed down with them. Even that traveling bag was getting a little heavy. It was time to let all of that go, and what better place than in the wonderful Endless. And, who knows? Maybe my bag needed to fly away just as I have done."

He smiled at Anthony. "But I do need to write down your address once again, Anthony. My address book was in the bag."

Straightening up, Mr. Watchit reached under his yellow raincoat and into one of those many pockets. "Look here!" He produced his battered bird book and his binoculars. "I did not lose these old friends. Or you. All of you. I did not lose you."

"And we... *hic*... we... *hic*... did not... lose you... *hic*... Mr. Watchit," smiled Anthony, his words jerking through the hiccups which usually signaled the end of his crying.

CHAPTER 24

Finally! The OUATs!

Anthony looked again at the steep hill rising right behind the boat dock. It was part of a chain of wooded hills forming this high side of the Endless. Extending as far as he could see, up river and down, these hills reminded him of pictures of the Loch Ness Monster. Now he understood why he saw just a few campfires the night before. These hills were in the way. This nearest hill right behind them was the one they would climb.

A worn path began just off the dock and disappeared quickly into a tangle of trees and brush. Tracing a possible route up the hill, Anthony imagined climbing to the top and looking down to see the OUATs camped in the valley below.

"It won't take you any time," Ratty had said earlier, pointing to the path's beginning and then sitting down on the dock to visit with Mr. Watchit and Pteros Chronos.

The rain had stopped, and a brilliant sunset was forming in the west. Anthony's companions had been watching the skies clear of the day's muddy clouds. They were in no hurry, chatting and laughing, thanking Ratty for his hospitality and his safe delivery of them to this side of the river. They even chanced a few small jokes about Mr. Watchit's balancing act, though no one mentioned the brown traveling bag.

Now would have been a perfect time for a cup of that raspberry tea and apricot scones or little ham biscuits that Mr. Watchit would carefully unwrap and share on the yellow tablecloth. A silence settled among them as they sensed the loss of that bag and all it had meant to them. Ratty interrupted the quiet with talk of future boating lessons for Mr. Watchit and the possibility of borrowing his friend Toad's new sailboat.

"And swimming lessons, Watchit. We should start there." Ratty's voice always carried the sound of hope, of happiness, as if everything were possible.

But Anthony was impatient with their conversation. He had been pacing the dock, checking on the condition of the steep path they would climb, wondering why he was the only one eager to begin. He joined them again but remained standing, hopeful his posture would signal his readiness to go. Besides, what did Ratty mean by "it won't take you any time"?

It *was* taking Time. They were taking Time. Anthony wondered briefly if they were taking *his* Time or if they all shared this Time. He had heard his mother talk about "sharing your time," but what did that mean? Was Time something to share like pizza or his remote control airplane? Was there just Time, a sort of Capital Letter Time, which was somehow divided into different uses? And what about right now? Wasn't this particular time *the Time* to go?

He was lost in these thoughts when Ratty stood up and handed him a small piece of blue paper, folded once over, hiding the message inside but not the fancy-lettered name on the front. *Anthony.*

"So here is a bit of a poem for you, Anthony," he said shyly. "Just in the event I don't see you at the Gathering. Wrote it myself. I do that from time to time. Just for special friends. No need to read it now. Just stick it in your pocket for safekeeping. Save it for another rainy day."

"Thank you," Anthony said, smiling. He took the blue paper, folded it twice more, and slid it into his back pocket, but he was clearly *preoccupied* as he did this. His thoughts were on the OUATs, not Ratty's poem. Being so preoccupied, Anthony did not notice he was not paying attention. It was a bit of inattention that would cause him sadness later.

Preoccupied was a word Miss Quickett had taught Anthony. She had requested that he add it to his dictionary. It was #4.

Either Ratty did not notice, or he noticed but understood, having a fair measure of the same tendency himself. He said good-bye again, reminded Mr. Watchit of boating lessons, and jumped back into his boat.

"I'll be shoving off. Need to cross before dark. Good-bye again," and he tipped his hat to his friends and began the trip back across the Endless, now rippling with the red and golden waters of a mirrored sunset.

The three travelers waved back and shouted out their thanks and then watched as Ratty and the small boat grew smaller and smaller until they became a single speck far away in the wide water.

Ratty was right. It was a short hike to the top, and it took almost no time. But when they got there and looked down through the trees and the gathering darkness, Anthony realized he had not imagined quite enough.

For the very long valley was filled with the winking and blinking of hundreds of campfires, the sounds of laughter and fiddle music, of occasional cheers and applause, of whoops and hollers, and even the smells of things delicious.

The OUATs! Finally!

CHAPTER 25

Giant!

He didn't see the giant. In his hurry to meet the OUATs, Anthony dashed off down the trail, leaving Mr. Watchit and Pteros Chronos following behind. The daylight was fading quickly, and the forest edges were dark and thick. His eyes were on those campfires jeweling the valley just ahead. Anthony simply ran right past the giant.

He never saw the Birkenstock sandals, the hairy knees, the green plaid walking shorts, or the enormous purple t-shirt with William Shakespeare's face and the words *Write On*. He failed to notice the huge smiling face, the wire-rimmed glasses atop a very long nose, the neatly trimmed beard, and the tent-sized floppy ears. All of this was bending down toward a hurrying Anthony from the pines trees above. All of this he missed.

But when he heard that voice, he stopped.

"Anthony. Anthony." The booming call came from above, though someone familiar with giantspeak would have recognized a tenderness in the voice.

Anthony looked up, thinking he was being paged by a loudspeaker. And there he was! A giant! A smiling giant who knew his name!

"Oh...ohhhhhh...I, I did not see you, sir. Sir, Mr. Giant." Anthony was tilting backward now and wondering how to properly address a giant. He was a little nervous but also certain that this was a friendly giant. "I was hurrying, sir. I wasn't paying attention. I'm sorry. I don't want to miss the stories. They're telling stories in the valley. My friends..." Anthony's voice trailed off. It all sounded very muddled, and just as he glanced back at the trail, wondering when Pteros Chronos and Mr. Watchit would appear, they did.

Hoping to alert them, Anthony gestured wildly, his whole body signaling, "Stop!" and "Giant!" and "Look Up!" But his contortions, tickled the giant whose keen eyesight matched his size and his enormous laugh. A giant's laughter bursting from treetops and rumbling the ground is hard to miss.

Pteros Chronos and Mr. Watchit stopped immediately, and, looking up, they saw the giant's beaming face bending low and smiling warmly.

"Welcome! Welcome!" he bellowed. "We have been expecting you for days! We're greatly delighted you will be joining us in our celebration!"

Pteros Chronos flashed his best sort of brilliance, lighting up the area, including the giant's plaid walking shorts. Mr. Watchit bowed, possibly confusing giants with royalty, though it was a gracious gesture and one the giant seemed to appreciate.

"I do have a bit of a speech, which I deliver to all our guests." The giant said this casually as he stepped right over the pine trees, watching out, of course, for Anthony and his friends, and then bending over and resting very large hands on his very hairy knees. "Now then, I must begin with a little story. This is the story of many stories. Stories upon stories. Stories multiplying and dividing and stories stacked and collected and treasured and stored and shared and...oh my, I get carried away. You see, we OUATs are story characters. We were born in stories, we are nurtured by stories, we live by stories. So, these gatherings, which go on in all sorts of places all the time, are filled with stories. But...excuse me for just a bit, please, while I...ugggg..." The giant straightened up, rumbling the ground a bit. "It's my back," he groaned. "Comes from being around so many little people. I'm forever stooping. Just give me a minute while I straighten myself." There were some loud cracks and popping sounds as the giant bent one way, then another. "Ahhh...that's better," and he bent down once more, his voice considerably softer. "Now, where was I?"

"Stories!" said Anthony. His eyes were big, bright. "You were telling us about the OUATs and how you share your stories."

"Yes, yes, yes. We do love this sharing, and we know these stories help us understand ourselves and even our enemies a little better. We know stories inspire us to do great, heroic acts, despite the odds. They help us learn what it means to be unselfish and how to use our wits and what love looks like. They encourage us to dream, to imagine. I, personally, love those stories best—the ones that encouraged me to imagine myself, a brutish sort of fellow, as a leader of literary gatherings. And here I am, doing just that!" The giant smiled his toothy smile and straightened back up, all but disappearing into the night sky.

"So, Mr. Giant," said Mr. Watchit, bowing slightly. "I am sadly unschooled in the stories of giants. Could you tell us who you are? I mean, from which story did you come?"

Anthony had already inventoried his list of giants. It was a short list—the beanstalk giant, the chasing giants, the selfish giant, and that big, friendly giant. Now, there was a possibility. Perhaps this was that giant. What was his name? Mrs. Quickett had read that story to Anthony's class and they had clapped at the end.

The giant bent down again, hands back on his hairy knees, whiff of garlic surrounding him.

"I am Horace Rumpus III, son of Conrad and Victoria Bismark Rumpus, a family of old stock giants and distantly related to the legendary giants of Farbeyond. Perhaps you have heard of them?" He paused, but there was no response from his audience. "But as a story character," he continued, "I am just a minor giant."

"A minor giant?" Anthony frowned, his eyebrows signaling a question. "How could you be called a minor giant?"

Explosions of gigantic laughter filled the air, shook the trees, rumbled the ground, and caused the travelers to lose their balance.

"Minor, Anthony, in a literary sense. I had a small role. It's doubtful you have ever read of me. I find that is often the case. For, you see, my story has been lost. It was called *The Good Giants of Yore*, a wonderful collection of old tales about the little-known good deeds giants have performed. No longer in print. Not one copy to be found." The giant's voice had dropped.

"I'm sorry, Mr. Horace Giant, truly sorry. That's just the sort of book my dad and I would love to read."

"Thank you, Anthony. My feelings exactly. That is why I am so dedicated to these OUAT gatherings. For, make no mistake, we story characters live in troubling times. Yes, this is an age of instant-this and immediate-that, and there is the possibility that the very art of telling stories and even of listening to stories is at risk. We do not want to be characters who lived only once. And so we gather together and we share. We save the stories. We carry the story torch."

It was an emotional speech, and the giant seemed winded and a little teary. He took a deep breath, and the travelers waited quietly for him to collect himself.

"Well," he cleared his throat in a rumbly sort of way, " I must say I am delighted to meet all of you. We are so happy you have come our way. Though now I should explain a few guidelines. You'll find it quite easy to lose yourself in all of these stories, Anthony, and I know you are on a mission."

For just a split second Anthony wondered what the giant meant by "mission." Even before reaching the valley filled with OUAT storytellers, he had momentarily forgotten his airplane.

"Pteros Chronos and Mr. Watchit, I suggest you each go your own way when we reach the campfires. You will be welcomed with great hospitality in any circle. One is as good as the next, though the stories are different. You may just listen to the stories, or, if you want, you may share a story. Plan to meet Anthony at Sunup at the Wordery. It's the white tent in the middle of the field. Then you can discuss plans for the day ahead. Anthony, you follow me. Just don't travel too close. I sometimes stop quite abruptly."

CHAPTER 26

Carry the Torch! Listen for the Story!

F ollowing a giant is tricky business. In fact, unless you are invited to do so, it is nearly impossible. For giants move quickly, and despite their bulk and the general notion that they are clumsy, they are quite agile and exceedingly strong. They don't give out. They can cover twenty-five miles in a matter of minutes. *The Guinness Book of Giant Records* (also sadly out of print) has recorded distance races of five hundred miles finished in well under an hour. Giants kick up dust, stones, parts of trees and bushes, creating a certain wake as they pass and clouding their tracks. Visibility for anyone following becomes limited. Each giant footstep exerts such impact upon the earth that, regardless of the care taken by certain giants to walk gently, the rumbly ground ripples outward from every heavy step, and traveling on moving ground is never easy.

All of this was, of course, new to Anthony. He had never read of anyone following a giant. He had never even imagined it. And though Horace Rumpus appeared to be one of those gentle giants, Anthony quickly realized that the problem was not following too closely but just keeping up.

Keeping up was all he could do. His legs were short and so became his breath. The dark and the dust and the campfire smoke made seeing the giant difficult, so he listened for the thudding steps. He felt for the vibrations. Mr. Watchit and Pteros Chronos had disappeared into the circles of storytellers. Anthony was following this giant alone.

Horace walked along the edges of the gathering, making every effort not to disturb the storytellers. Anthony followed somewhere behind. But that passage, down into the valley and then along one side of the campfires, was, for Anthony, simply a blur, hazy and indistinct. Later he would remember seeing faces—children's faces, and firelight reflecting on those faces—and hearing the sounds of stories, just snippets really, rising like smoke into the night sky.

"He yelled for us to run to the tower..."

"We floated for months on the raft..."

"She was old and wrinkled and smoked a cigar..."

Mostly Anthony remembered that no one seemed to notice him struggling to keep up with the giant. No one noticed him at all. Everyone else was listening to stories while he was listening to the giant's heavy footfalls. Until suddenly they stopped.

Anthony stopped. He stood very still, waiting for the giant to reappear and for the dust to settle. In that Waiting Time, a beautiful thing happened that Anthony would not forget.

As he watched, the dust particles began to twirl and glitter. Suspended in the night air and reflecting the firelight, they drifted downward in a spangled shower of light all around him. Anthony stretched out his arms, trying to catch the pieces of glorious light.

"It's like my snow globe. It's just like my snow globe," Anthony called out to anyone who might be listening. "Look at this! I'm in a snow globe!"

The snow globe had belonged to his mother when she was Anthony's age, but she had given it to him. It was his favorite Christmas ornament. He loved unwrapping it every year and rediscovering his wish to join the tiny carolers under the tiny streetlight of that tiny village with snow falling on them. He thought about the old green trunk in the attic where he and his mother had carefully wrapped the snow globe in newspaper and packed it away with the other ornaments.

Anthony was quite suddenly homesick. He remembered his mother saying the snow globe would be waiting for him throughout the whole year.

"No matter where you go, Anthony, the carolers will be here." That's exactly what his mother had said to him.

"No matter where I go?" Anthony asked aloud now, repeating the words inside his head. "No matter where I go. Even here, in this valley, following a..."

The giant's smiling face suddenly appeared above him.

"Glorious, isn't it?" Horace said gently. "This dust-catching light, simply glorious. As if heaven is sifting down on us, bit by bit. But it does take noticing. Many people never see it. And that's a shame indeed. I'm glad you noticed, Anthony." The giant paused and together they watched as the glittery light drifted all around them.

"No matter where I go..." Anthony could almost hear his mother speak those words.

It would be years later, when Anthony was a grown man, before he understood the strength those words had given him on this adventure. For the power of a promise to wait—to be constant, to remain, no matter what—is never just a matter of words, no matter where you go.

"Well," said the giant finally, quietly. "If you are ready, Anthony, I'd like to introduce you. Be quite still, and I'll just ... " Anthony felt himself suddenly cradled in one of the giant's hands and swooshed upward. Way, way up. When Horace opened his hand, Anthony, who had never been bothered by heights, crept to the edge of the giant's palm to see the whole of the valley winking with campfires. And there! Spread out below him and filling the valley were the OUATs!

"Now then, Anthony," said Horace. "If you would be ever so kind as to stand very still. And you might want to cover your ears. I may be a bit loud." The giant cupped his free hand to his lips while extending his other arm. Anthony held tightly to the giant's thumb. "Please excuse the interruption," Horace bellowed. Instantly the whole valley fell silent. "I want to introduce Anthony Bartholomew Mandopolis of the Lost Airplane."

The OUATs below exploded in cheers, and when Anthony looked down again, his eyes caught a small flashing light from one of the campfires below.

"Dot, dot, dot," the light blinked. "All's well," the light blinked.

"No matter where you go," Anthony whispered to himself.

After the cheering ended, the giant continued. "Anthony and his companions, Mr. Exactus Watchit and Pteros Chronos, have journeyed here in hopes of finding that airplane. If you have any information regarding the whereabouts of this vehicle, please meet

Anthony at Sunup tomorrow at the Wordery. And now, shall we continue? Carry the Torch! Listen for the Story!"

As Anthony was gently lowered to the ground, a huge cry echoed from the OUATs. "Carry the Torch! Listen for the Story!"

The giant deposited him near a circle of OUATs who graciously made room for him between a very round woman quite bundled in a green and brown camouflage cape and a thin, old man who was smoking an enormous pipe. They smiled at Anthony and both whispered, "Carry the Torch! Listen for the Story!" as if they spoke some kind of password for the next story that was about to begin.

That storyteller was standing on the far side of the campfire, and Anthony saw that everyone in the circle was watching him and waiting. He was a wild-looking man with spikes of red hair poking out from under a wide-brimmed cowboy hat. A faded bandana was tied around his neck, his legs were covered by leather chaps, and his boots were outfitted with real spurs. He was the kind of character Anthony's grandmother might call a *ruffian*, and she might be right, especially now that Anthony could see that twined around his shoulders was a huge rattlesnake.

The thin, old man leaned in close. "Raised by coyotes," he whispered.

The camouflage-covered lady nodded her head and winked at Anthony. "He's called Bill," she whispered.

"Good to have you here, little buckaroo," said the cowboy, nodding in Anthony's direction. The snake hissed.

"Yessiree! I'm a rootin' tootin' cowboy, glad to be here with all ya'll folks again. Yep, yep, this here campfire shore brings a cowboy home. Yep. Makes me plumb glad I left Cal-e-forn-i-a. " The snake nodded its head. The audience clapped and whistled. "Yessiree, when I left Cal-e-forn-i-a, that there dust storm blew so wicked that they lost half that state to Arizona. Yep, yep. Now that ditch they call the Grand Canyon is plumb filled up with California dust. Yep, yep."

Bill the cowboy told more stories about lassoing a tornado and taming a grizzly bear, and he even promised Anthony he'd be on the lookout for that airplane the next time he was traveling on a lightning bolt.

The circle of listeners laughed and clapped, and the snake looped and twisted around the cowboy's neck, seeming to smile at the audience.

Later, when Anthony would return home and tell his friends about meeting the real Pecos Bill and his tame rattlesnake, they would laugh.

"Yep," they'd say. "Sorta like you met Robin Hood? You wouldn't be exaggerating again, would you, Anthony?"

CHAPTER 27

Stories Upon Stories

Anthony spent that whole night in the company of wizards and cowboys, pirates and poets, dwarves and dragons, rascals, heroes, dreamers, and some ordinary children on adventures just like him. He listened, he laughed, he held his breath at close escapes. He traveled through the desert and wondered which way to go, his heart hurt with sadness. He cheered when battles were won, and, when it was his time, he shared his own story. When each story ended, Anthony joined a chorus of applause and repeated the words, "Carry the Torch! Listen for the Story!"

It was surprising to Anthony that so many children were present in this circle, in all the circles. Some of them were OUATs, he was sure of that, but many were guests just like him. He turned to ask the camouflage lady about this, but she had quietly disappeared.

Anthony turned to the thin old man sitting to his right. Perhaps he would know.

Now Anthony saw that the man was dressed in homespun britches and a patched shirt, covered by a cracked leather vest. His boots were worn and muddy, and the frayed laces were knotted in several places. In addition to the pipe, he clutched a small green velvet bag drawn together by a golden cord, an accessory of high quality that seemed unlikely in his crooked fingers. His skin was pale, his head was bald, and a great gray beard bristled and curled around his chin. He was sitting cross-legged and so very still that Anthony hesitated to bother him. But they were between stories, and the circle was resettling. It was a good time to ask.

"Sir? Excuse me, sir. I was wondering about all these children I see here. There are lots of children." Anthony began shyly, knowing he was one of 'these children.' "I mean, where do they come from? How do they get here? I got here through the Boulders."

The old man had turned to face him. He smiled and his eyes disappeared into the crinkles of that smile. "Yes. I heard that in your story. Rock portals are often passageways, though not without danger. I'm sure you know that, Anthony." His voice sounded rusty, like an old gate hinge.

Anthony nodded, though he could not quite remember any dangers. Pteros Chronos had kept him safe.

"Yours is a wonderful question and one which has many answers." The old man paused to uncross his legs and generally rearrange himself. He took so much time that Anthony wondered if he had forgotten the question.

"There are endless entrances to this world," he finally creaked. "Though you must be looking closely. You must be observant. It appears that children are the most attentive to these magical places. Sometimes it is simply by opening a door . . . to an attic or a closet or an empty room with a wardrobe. Sometimes it's by walking through a gate, crossing a bridge, or holding onto a key or a ring or a sword or the neck of a unicorn or the mane of a lion. Sometimes it's by planting magic beans."

He shook the green bag close enough that Anthony heard a delicate clinking sound inside. "You, my boy, are evidence that climbing through boulders or even just sitting on a rock can bring you here. I suppose one could travel here from almost any place. That is, of course, if one had a yearning for such travel." The old man stopped and drew deeply on his pipe.

"Oh, and by the way, Mrs. X will be back. She flies away now and again. She would want me to include skydoors in my list of portals into this lovely place." The man smiled and turned back to wait for the next story.

Later in the night a large, bearded man with a guitar stood to sing. He introduced himself as a *troubadour*, a word that made Anthony bunch up his eyebrows.

Mrs. X, who had returned, without his notice, with gauzy layers of purple and turquoise capes floating around her neck, leaned close to Anthony and whispered, "Troubadour. That's an old word for a traveling singer. He sings his stories."

Anthony nodded. He whispered troubadour several times, loving the way the word felt in his mouth. "He's like a caroler," he whispered back, thinking of the tiny carolers waiting for him in the green trunk. Later he would add troubadour to his dictionary. He would put a star beside it and the words *Mrs. X*.

As the troubadour sang about a sweetheart across the sea, Anthony stretched out and looked up at the wide night sky. There was no sign of Polaris, but there was something, many somethings, thin and floating, suspended from somewhere high above him. Like threads, they were lengthening and shortening and winding, mostly invisible but now and then catching the firelight. Anthony waited until the song ended and a stretching break followed, and then he asked Mrs. X about them.

"Oh, yesssss," she smiled. Her eyes were large and happy behind the thick-framed glasses. "You noticed.

Well done, Anthony. That is a wonderful story, too. So here we are—storytellers gathered together to share our stories. But, beyond this sharing, we also want to preserve these stories. That makes us *preservationists,* too. That's another good word, Anthony. It means those who want to keep something safe, something preserved." She paused again, somewhat dramatically, knowing that the real question Anthony wanted answered was not yet answered. It is an old storytelling technique, especially impressive with multiple capes. "That's what's going on up there." Mrs. X looked up, squinting her eyes into tiny slits. "Thousands of spiders. You can't see them, but they are up there somewhere, busy spinning their silk threads and then recording our stories. It's a kind of *encoding* . . . do you know that word, Anthony? Encoding?" She paused, looking back at Anthony. Her eyes were round again. It was a serious question.

He nodded, though his head was upturned still, and his eyes squinted into the dark sky. *Encoding* was a word he had learned from a cereal box contest. He had to create a code and use it to write a sentence. That was encoding. It seemed a long time ago. Now, as he watched the thin strands of silk float and wave about and disappear into the upper stretches of night air, he wondered about the tiny spiders who encoded silk threads with stories.

"But, Mrs. X, what are the threads attached to? Don't they need a platform, something to hang from?"

"Oh, my goodness! You are a clever boy. Yes, they do need something. I believe it's called a skyhook. Now that's a something I have never encountered in all the flying I have done. But, you know spiders are terribly creative architects, and these particular spiders, all of them, are the descendants of an old family of writers as well. Encoding is easy for them. The whole system of encoding has been streamlined and now is quite technical. Not the sort of work for just any spider. As you well know, not all spiders are literate."

Anthony nodded again. His neck was aching from this position, but he so wanted to see the spiders. "How does the encoding work on spider silk?" he asked.

"I'm afraid some of the process remains a mystery to me. I do know that every single word of every story told here is recorded on silk, wound tightly into a story sac, much like a cocoon, Anthony, and then stored in abandoned wasp nests. It seems there is an abundance of those, and they are simply perfect containers for our stories. Which makes us recyclers, too, I suppose." Mrs. X chuckled.

"We recycle too," Anthony remarked, thinking about the recycling bins on the back porch and wondering who was taking them and the garbage to the curb in his absence.

"The Story Nests—that's what we call them—are carefully labeled and then taken to the dwarves who have an elaborate storage system in their caves. Climate controlled, of course. A group of seven brothers is in charge of storage. It's a cooperative endeavor, my dear boy. The caves are open for visitors with comfortable plushy chairs, though they are a bit small, and little tables, just like a library."

"And even my story, the one I told tonight, even that story is recorded?" Anthony's eyes were large with the thought.

"Oh my, yes. Every single word of it. You see, Anthony, all stories have importance." She glanced around the circle of storytellers. Someone had added wood to the fire, and the circle was seated again, quietly awaiting the next story. Without any cue, the group spoke the words, now so familiar to Anthony, "Carry the Torch! Listen for the Story!"

With the help of a staff, an ancient man wrapped in a gray cloak arose. Anthony had watched him throughout the night, for he was seated on the far side of the fire, apart from the circle. All night he had remained so still that he could have been mistaken for a big rock. His face was almost hidden within the folds of a heavy hood, but his eyes flashed. When he began his story, a flurry of unexpected wind whipped all around him, sparking the fire.

"Once upon a time," the man spoke in a voice deep and thunderous, and lightning flashed in the distance, "...before the naming of England, there was, in the land, a great need of a great king. This is the story of that king and the knights who served him."

Anthony glanced upward at the unseen spiders who were encoding every single word.

CHAPTER 28

Sunup

Sunup! That's what Anthony was thinking about. And the Wordery. That, too. The giant had been clear.

"Meet at the Wordery at Sunup," he had said.

The darkness had thinned to a silvery gray sky. The campfires had burned down, leaving wispy trails of smoke curling in the early morning air. The stories had been shared and spun and stored in their silken nests, and the OUATs were sleepy. Some were already fast asleep, as was their custom after a night of storytelling.

Anthony had never before stayed awake all night long, but he wasn't sleepy. He was too excited. And anxious. He watched the eastern hills. Very soon the sun would burst over those hills and it would be Sunup! He didn't have much time to find the Wordery.

He turned to Mrs. X. She had taken off her pink ballet slippers and was unwinding some of the long capes and shaping them into a pillow. Now Anthony realized that much of her roundness was due to the layer upon layer of capes. Standing before him now, she appeared as a very small woman with a mass of curls. Purple curls today, he noticed. She smiled and yawned at Anthony, all at the same time.

"Find yourself a cozy spot, Anthony. We sleep until Sundown. Then we begin again with more stories." She smiled and yawned again. "I'll be sure to wake you." Then she turned back to plump her pillow.

"But, Mrs. X," Anthony's voice had an unnatural sound to it. Mrs. X was accustomed to hearing all manner of unnatural sounds. She immediately stopped folding her capes and faced him with her full attention. "Mrs. X," he repeated. "I'm supposed to meet my friends Pteros Chronos and Mr. Watchit at the Wordery at Sunup. The giant, Horace Rumpus, said so. But I don't..." and there was a long sigh and a lifting of his shoulders and wobble in the words that followed, "I don't know where the Wordery is, and I'm afraid I won't be there on time."

Mrs. X instantly hurried over to Anthony on her unmatched stocking feet. "Oh, my dear boy! There, there. Not to worry!" She bent very close to Anthony and held him gently by his shoulders, and he could see behind her thick glasses were deep violet eyes, maybe even purple. Her sweet breath smelled of licorice. "Anthony, I shall point you in the direction of the Wordery. It's the only white tent in the valley. But it won't be a straight path. Few paths are straight. You must expect turns and roundabouts. Detours even." She turned him a quarter of a circle and pointed. "There! Do you see that sleeping dragon just this side of the lacy tree?"

"Yes," Anthony nodded.

"You are to walk between that dragon and that bundle of small people." Mrs. X took off her glasses and squinted. "They are either dwarves or hobbits. I can't tell from here, but don't *ever* say I said that. As different as cabbages from periwinkles, they are, and mighty proud of themselves. Now as for Sunup." Mrs. X faced the rosy east and spread her arms wide in a huge inhale of the coming day. She paused. She breathed in and out, in and out. "Oh the glory of Sunup. But, Anthony, it's not possible to be late for Sunup. Sunup is not an exact time, my boy. It's delightfully imprecise. Sunup flows. We here observe heavenly time periods...Sunup and Sundown. Night and day. Morning and evening. Those words are enough for us. Minutes make me very nervous." She chuckled and gave Anthony a quick squeeze and then whispered, "Carry the torch. Listen for the Story."

Then she vanished. Her slippers, her cape pillow, her glasses, all of her. Gone. In an instant.

Anthony smiled as he headed toward the sleeping dragon. He thought about Mrs. X and how she was the only one in their circle who had not told a story.

"Pass on by me," she had said, fluttering her hand in a tiny gesture of impatience. The old man had told Anthony that she was a mystery writer.

"Uses a *pseudonym*, as well as capes," he had whispered.

Much later Anthony would learn what pseudonym means, though for a long time he thought it referred to some flying device. He would enter it into his dictionary with another star for Mrs. X, mystery writer.

CHAPTER 29

Directions

As Mrs. X had warned, there was no real path to the Wordery. Anthony had to make his own, tip-toeing around and stepping over creatures and characters who were sprawled about or curled up. They were fast asleep, and most were snoring. Rings of orange and crimson smoke puffed regularly from the dozing dragon. Anthony's passage was no interruption.

It was as if some magic had visited the valley, like the enchantment that fell upon the whole castle in *Sleeping Beauty*. Anthony was thinking about that story, about that prince whose kiss awakened the princess and then the kingdom. He was thinking how glad he was that this sleeping was just ordinary sleeping and that no kissing would be required of him, when he saw the white tent of the Wordery and a familiar bobbing light beside the tall figure of Mr. Watchit.

Anthony was excited and relieved to see his friends again. He had so much to tell them. Apparently Pteros Chronos and Mr. Watchit felt the same, for they greeted one another with lights flashing and a boisterous enthusiasm, and all three friends began talking at once, all telling stories of their experiences among the OUATs.

Pteros Chronos, his light blazing in all directions in a sort of nervous brilliance, told Anthony that he had met Alice. What's more, Alice and two other OUATs were waiting to speak with him about the airplane. "There," he said, swooping his beam to the shadowed side of the Wordery tent where three figures leaned against the tent in several postures of weariness. "Alice has information for you, just as Ratty said. I am not certain about the others. They simply appeared here. Perhaps they heard the giant's request and are here to help. They are waiting to speak with you."

But Mr. Watchit, who seemed almost transformed by his night among the OUATs, interrupted Pteros Chronos in a most uncustomary way. He appeared unable to wait his turn to speak. "I have never heard such stories, Anthony! And, do you know about the spiders? And the hobbits. Do you know about the hobbits? I met a hobbit, a Mr. Bilbo Baggins, a fine fellow who lives in a hole in the ground with a round door—all hobbits have round doors. And I met Toad, Ratty's friend. He invited me to visit him." Mr. Watchit paused just briefly to catch his breath.

"And this Wordery! An amazement! Do you know the bakers here bake cookies and scones from words. Muffins too. All out of words, Anthony. I have just eaten a PETROUS cookie. Well, not all of it. Petrous means hard, stony and it did taste remarkably like gravel. But, I was drawn to it because the word Petrous is so close to Pteros, who we know to be our winged friend and guide. Just the slightest change in the letters E and T and the last minute addition of a U and we can change from glorious flight to a hard stone." Mr. Watchit paused and smiled at this lesson he had just shared.

Anthony smiled too. "So, do you think the bakers at the Wordery could make a cookie called MUD? Or GARBAGE? Or . . ." but he wasn't able to finish. The giggles interrupted.

"Well, Anthony, there are many choices of nourishments," Mr. Watchit continued in his serious voice, ignoring the peals of laughter now exploding from Anthony. "But here, Anthony," he pulled a brown paper bag from one of his pockets. "I've selected some cookies for you from the Wordery. For your journey."

"Thank you, Mr. Watchit. We can share them." Anthony forced his lips together in an effort to keep the tickles on the inside. Mostly he succeeded.

Sensing a pause in Mr. Watchit's speech, Pteros Chronos expanded again to include Alice and the two other OUATs who were now sitting down on the grass. They squinted in his light.

"Now," he said, whirring his multiple wings in a hovering position, "we must consider the time and our friends here who have come to help. They are quite sleepy. We must hear from them before they nod off. Let me present Alice to you, Anthony."

Alice got up, dusted herself off, and curtsied.

"So very nice to meet you, Anthony," she said with some effort. It was obvious she had been napping and was trying hard to speak as though she hadn't. "Well," she began, lifting of her small shoulders as if to indicate a long story to follow, "it was really the white rabbit who saw the event. He was to accompany me here, this morning, but I lost track of him somewhere along the way.

"Well," she repeated, rolling her eyes upward as if her story existed somewhere in the sky. "It seems," she yawned and sighed and looked back at Anthony. "It seems that the airplane floated past the rabbit several days ago, as he walked along the river path. Hmmm, now that I think of it, this occurred in the late afternoon. He was returning to this very gathering, upriver from here. He was traveling along the path and noticed this floating object.

"He knew it was not a boat, not a fish or a bird, and that it would not last long if it stayed upon the water." She yawned again. "Even from the bank he could tell it was constructed from paper.

"So he got a large branch and hurried downstream to await its coming. Just as he had snagged the object, which we do believe was your airplane…just at that moment of capture, and as he was pulling it to shore with the help of the branch, one of those magpies swooped right down, picked up the plane in its beak, and flew south, following the river for as long as the rabbit could see."

She yawned yet again. "He was really quite cross with the incident. It made him late for the storytelling, and he had nothing to show for it." Alice paused and took a big breath, which brought on a series of yawns.

"So," Mr. Watchit stepped closer to Alice. He wanted to boil down this rather jumbled story to just the information Anthony needed. "So, the airplane was taken from the river by the magpie who flew south, following the river?"

"Yes, precisely," yawned Alice.

"Do you know any more, Alice?" questioned Pteros Chronos, shining his light directly on her.

"No," she said, sitting down and hugging her knees to her chest in a position that seemed intended to keep her awake.

"It seems to me that we will have to use logic here, for there are some pieces missing in this puzzle." Another girl stepped out of the shadows and introduced herself as Nancy. She had straight blond hair and eyes the same blue as Mr. Watchit's. She smiled when she spoke.

"I seem to have some ability in solving mysteries, and I wanted to help you, Anthony," the new girl said.

"We know the magpies operate a trading post downriver. It's quite a large establishment really, and has been in operation for years. The magpies often acquire their goods from the Endless. The river has a continual supply of floating things, after all. The magpies arrange and display these items so that they appear to have a new quality. They sell and trade them. It's recycling, and it benefits all, even the river. It gives the magpies a reason to gather together and, well, to visit. I believe your airplane, Anthony, has landed at the Magpie Trading Post. I also believe it will not be there long. Airplanes are not among their usual selection." She smiled the whole time she spoke, as if finding the airplane was not a problem but a grand adventure.

"Do you know where this trading post is?" asked Anthony, squinting his eyes in a way that sometimes helped him concentrate, and certainly made him look very serious.

"That's where I can help." The boy in the threesome had politely waited until last to speak. He was dressed in leggings and thick stockings, and he wore scuffed black shoes with buckles. His eyes were bright and his long, brown hair was thick and tangled. He held out his hand to Anthony. "My name's Jim. Jim Hawkins. I've drawn up this map for you."

Anthony felt the strong grip of Jim's handshake and, as he unrolled a cracked piece of parchment, saw that Jim's hands were rough and scarred. Pteros Chronos concentrated a light directly on the map.

"Wow!" exclaimed Anthony, looking now at the map. "This looks like a pirate's map!"

Jim smiled. "Well, I suppose you could say that's where I got my training." Mr. Watchit and Pteros Chronos both crowded close as Jim pointed out landmarks and directions and explained a route that began at the Wordery and ended with a red X at the Magpie Trading Post.

"I'd go across country, Anthony. The Endless has a great curve in it. You'll save time if you travel across these hills, going due east." Jim pointed to the river's curve on the map. "You may arrive before noon, if you start now."

"Thank you. Thank you, all of you," said Mr. Watchit, though Alice and now Nancy were both asleep, and Jim was already busy attaching a hammock to nearby tree limbs.

"Yes, thank you. I won't forget you," said Anthony, holding the map and looking again at this friendly, helpful boy named Jim who had learned mapmaking from pirates.

Anthony, Pteros Chronos, and Mr. Watchit continued studying the map, noting the parting of trees in the horizon of eastern hills. There, they decided, was where they would cross over. It matched the route Jim had suggested.

Pteros Chronos had already begun whirring in that direction when they were startled by a voice, somewhat frantic in nature.

"Anthony! Anthony! Oh, I'm so glad I made it in time. Toto disappeared, and I have spent all this time searching for him."

A girl slightly older than Anthony gasped these words. It was clear she had been running and was quite out of breath. The small whiskered dog she held was the Toto she had chased down. He smiled as dogs will do and was not in the least bit breathless.

For a moment she simply stood still, collecting herself and catching her breath, until Pteros Chronos, aware of time escaping, prompted her.

"And you have information regarding Anthony's airplane?" he asked.

"Oh, no. No information. I just remember a time when I was setting out on a great adventure, and the Good Witch of the North gave me this for protection."

And she leaned down and very gently kissed a very wide-eyed Anthony on his forehead. "There," she said. "You are traveling with special good magic, Anthony. Carry the Torch! Listen for the Story! Oh, my, I'm awfully glad we made it in time."

Anthony watched as she turned and walked quietly back through the clusters and bunches of sleeping OUATs. Toto gazed over her shoulder at Anthony, who had been around dogs enough to recognize a dog's good-bye when he saw one.

Gently he touched the kissed spot on his forehead, but he didn't wipe it off.

CHAPTER 30

Goodbyes

Morning shadows stretched across the valley. The only movement was that of Anthony, Pteros Chronos, and Mr. Watchit, who twisted and turned their way through the sleeping OUATs and toward the eastern rise of hills. There they would find an ancient trail, which, according to Jim's map, would lead them through a pass and then down on the other side to the Magpie's Trading Post. It had been a silent departure from the company of the OUATs. Anthony was thinking how quickly that time with them had passed. He wished he had said proper goodbyes.

By the time they had climbed to that break in the tree line, they were winded. The view alone suggested a rest, for they were at the narrow gap between two thickly wooded hills, just as the map showed. Distances stretched out with views of what lay ahead of them and what they were leaving behind.

Mr. Watchit provided small tin cups, a thermos of raspberry tea, and apple scones, all from the Wordery and carried in one of his pockets. He set the refreshments out under the shade of trees, though his movements were sharp and jerky and his usual happy humming did not accompany his activity. Had Anthony been paying attention, he would have noticed that Mr. Watchit's silence signaled something important.

They gathered quietly. They spoke of the good trail so far and how helpful it was to have Jim's map, and Anthony asked questions about magpies and if they were friendly birds and related to crows. However, there seemed no spirit to their talk. Their conversation felt forced and awkward, and their silences were uncomfortable.

Finally Mr. Watchit, looking directly at Anthony and then at Pteros Chronos, spoke. Anthony would forever after remember this moment and the blueness of Mr. Watchit's eyes.

"I'd like to speak with you, Anthony and Pteros Chronos... about a decision I have made. It has been a hard decision, and I find now it is hard to even say aloud. But I must." Mr. Watchit paused and took a deep breath. Anthony stopped, his cup of tea halfway to his mouth. Pteros Chronos stopped, his light dimming, his wings still.

"I won't be going any farther," said Mr. Watchit, turning his head from side to side as if he needed help in saying this. "I came this far because I wanted to speak to you privately. I've decided to remain here with the OUATs."

And now everything stopped. There was no sound of birdsong, no wind through the trees, no movement of cloud overhead. Like a photograph, they were locked in place, silent and motionless.

Finally Mr. Watchit spoke again, his voice soft, gentle. "You have been my best friends. In all of my life, I have never had friends such as the two of you. Even though our friendship is somewhat short as lifetimes go, I'm not sure I ever will again meet up with friends like you.

"But, you see, we are fast approaching the end of the journey. That is, this particular journey. You and Pteros Chronos will find your airplane, and then you will return to your family. Pteros Chronos will go back to his. I will be left, unable to continue with either of you."

There was a long pause here as Mr. Watchit handed Anthony a handkerchief and Anthony blew loudly into it. "I have found a family here, you see, among the OUATs. I have never even imagined this sort of family—so varied, so affirming, so accepting of one another. I have made so many friends already. Ratty and Toad and Mr. Baggins. All of them have invited me to visit.

"And the Endless. I never want to leave this river. And the Wordery! The chief baker there reminds me of my own grandmother. She has asked me to help her. Her past experience is mostly making gingerbread men, but she is learning, and she thinks I can learn, too. We will bake words into nourishments. What could be better than a job making cookies from words! I would even have an apron—with pockets." He smiled at Anthony though tears were streaming down his cheeks and off his long nose.

For just a bit of time, all three of them cried, even Pteros Chronos in a light-flickering, sputtering, and blinking cry that was somehow a comfort to the group. For, as Anthony learned that day, there is something binding about crying together. He viewed Pteros Chronos differently after watching him cry, though he secretly wondered if some electrical circuit controlled both his speech and his brilliance, and crying resulted in a crossing of wires.

But their crying was short-lived. The friends dried their eyes and blew their noses and finished the scones Mr. Watchit had brought. Anthony's scone was labeled *Pretense*. It appeared to be made with chocolate pieces, but those turned out to be dark prunes, and there was nothing chocolate about it. Pteros Chronos explained that pretense meant pretending to be something you are not and later, at home, Anthony would add that word to his dictionary with the small notation 'prune scone from the Wordery.'

Clearing up was quiet and too quick. Suddenly it was time to say good-bye. Anthony felt he could not bear saying those words to this friend, though he knew Mr. Watchit's decision was right and good.

Mr. Watchit handed him another brown sack. "Here, some muffins from the Wordery," he said. "I tried to select words I felt would help you along the way."

"Certainly they will, Mr. Watchit," said Pteros Chronos, who was making every effort to brighten up. "I will ask for you when I come back to this valley. We will meet again."

"Yes. Indeed. Thank you, Pteros Chronos. Thank you for including me in this amazing adventure. I will never ever forget it." Suddenly Mr. Watchit picked up Anthony and twirled him around and around. His father did that, and it was impossible not to laugh. Even now. Mr. Watchit laughed, too, and so did Pteros Chronos. "Thank you, Anthony," he said, putting him back down. "You listened for my story. You listened when I did not even know I had a story."

Mr. Watchit lifted his safari hat off his head and swooped it down and across his knees, bowing. "Carry the Torch. Listen for the Story," he said, smiling, straightening himself back to his full height and looking long at Anthony.

Then he turned and headed back down to the valley. Anthony heard him humming.

CHAPTER 31

The Magpie Trading Post

"I forgot the torch. I forgot to get the torch!" Anthony spoke these words in a whispery, anxious voice and only to himself. Pteros Chronos was too far ahead to hear him. They had been walking, mostly in silence, for more than an hour and both were feeling limp after Mr. Watchit's unexpected good-bye. The gap between them widened as Pteros Chronos kept to his usual brisk pace and Anthony lagged behind. "I forgot to get the torch!" Anthony repeated, raising his voice to reach the bobbing light ahead. "I promised to carry the torch, Pteros Chronos, but I forgot to get it!"

Pteros Chronos turned around so quickly that rays of light separated slightly from his center in a spangly swish. "What's that, Anthony? What are you saying about the torch?" His light enlarged, filling the space between him and Anthony, who had stopped walking and was looking at Pteros Chronos with large, serious eyes.

"What should we do?" Anthony asked.

"Well, perhaps you forgot about the torch, but you did not leave it behind, Anthony. The torch is within you. It's the light we all carry. We are born with a light inside. Mine just happens to be quite visible." He paused here and shimmered. "Everyone has the torch, this inside light, though some forget to switch it on. Indeed I believe some have lost sight of the switch altogether. Others see it when you are kind or brave. 'Carry the Torch!' is a reminder to turn on the switch inside. Do not trouble yourself, Anthony. You have not forgotten the torch or the switch."

"You mean there is no *actual* torch?" Anthony's eyes squinted with the effort to understand.

"Well, I am not equipped to speak about what is actual. That, my boy, is a very tricky word. But, speaking of words—do you hear something? Listen. There. Do you hear that?"

Drifting up to them were bits and pieces of sound, like static on a radio. "I believe we are hearing the magpies, Anthony! Shall we hurry along?"

Hurry they did, all downhill to a stand of large leafy trees bordering the Endless, a comfort to see once again. Stationed in front of the trees was a sign on a tall post.

Magpie Trading Post
Welcome
WAIT HERE!

"I guess this is the actual trading post, Pteros Chronos," smiled Anthony.

"Yes. Indeed. The actual one."

Now, in addition to hearing bits and pieces of words, they saw bits and pieces of things hanging in a haphazard way from tree limbs or propped against tree trunks. Anthony spotted a bicycle wheel, boat paddles and a garden rake hanging from a near branch and a sunhat atop a bowling ball against a tree. Shiny beads or maybe fishing lures caught the sunlight. Flutterings of black-and-white wings busied through the branches, and a constant chatter filled the trees.

"...go haywire...in the nick of time...the end of your rope...I'd give my eye teeth for that...more than meets the eye for sure...you can bet your bottom dollar..."

While Anthony and Pteros Chronos waited, they scanned the area, identifying what they could see from where they stood. Later they would only remember seventeen things, though it was certain the Magpie's inventory continued well beyond their view and into the trees and along the banks of the river. What they saw included a broom, basketball, fishing lures, bits of rope, a tangle of mosquito netting, a birdcage, several baskets, jugs, a doghouse, an extension cord, a checkerboard, an umbrella, a bowling ball, a sunhat, a minnow bucket, fence posts, a park bench, unmatched shoes, an accordion, a picture frame, a garden shovel, a life preserver, a garbage pail, bottle caps, a packing crate, medicine bottles, a cracked hand mirror, toy boats, an outhouse, a serving tray, a rake, a coffeepot, bicycle wheels, notes in bottles, paddles, parts of paddles, and a kitchen sink.

While they waited, the chattering continued. It was hard to know if they were hearing several magpies at work among the trees or a single bird who was so busy talking that he had not noticed them.

Finally a very large black-and-white bird streaked with iridescent green swooped out of the trees, speaking as he landed. Anthony noticed a fancy wristwatch around the bird's neck and thought of Mrs. Quickett. For just a moment, he wondered what his friends were doing in that faraway classroom with all the timers and the angelfish swimming in the fish tank.

"Hello, hello, hello. Been here a while? Working behind the scenes, I am. Busy as a bee. Not a moment to lose. Hello, hello. I am your personal shopper and, might I add, the Trader of the Month. Wheeler Dealer, that's what I am. Call me Chester. Now, what do you have? Things to trade? What sort of things?"

"We are looking for an airplane," said Pteros Chronos, quickly aware of the need to be direct with Chester.

"An airplane you say. Do you mean something like a Cessna 172, a Lear Jet, a glider, a biplane, a helicopter, the grand Concorde, perhaps?"

"Oh no, no, no. I, that is, *we* are looking for a paper airplane," said Anthony.

"A paper airplane?" Chester cocked his head and looked first at Anthony, then at Pteros Chronos. "Whoever would fly in a paper airplane? Wonders never cease. Beats me. A paper airplane?"

"Well, it's not an airplane for flying in. It's actually a letter." Anthony looked at Pteros Chronos for help.

"A letter. Which letter? *A, B, C*?" Chester was fidgeting and clicking his beak impatiently.

"Let me explain," began Pteros Chronos in his teaching voice. "The airplane was constructed from a paper note. Not a musical note. A note of correspondence. We are searching for this paper airplane. A magpie was seen carrying it south from the upper Endless. It is of extreme importance that we find Anthony's paper airplane."

The magpie rolled his beady eyes upward and hummed a bit. He seemed to be going over his inventory.

"Could it be a paper airplane note which begins with the salutation, *Dear Mr. and Mrs. Mandopolis*?" asked Chester.

"Yes! That's it! That's my airplane!" The words burst from Anthony. "Do you have it?"

"No."

"No?"

"Yes. No. We did have it, that very airplane, but airplanes move along quickly. Finders keepers. Losers weepers."

"My airplane's gone? It was here and it's already gone?" Anthony looked from Chester to Pteros Chronos. His face fell. His shoulders fell. He sat down hard on the ground, covered his face with his hands, and curled himself into a small ball, which heaved with great, shaking sobs.

Pteros Chronos, immediately surrounding Anthony with light, spoke softly but firmly to him. "Hold fast, Anthony, my boy. You are quite tired now. Understandably tired. But, we will determine who has the airplane, and after we have rested, we will travel there. This is a mere setback, Anthony. Hold fast. There, there."

All the while Chester, quite alarmed by Anthony's tears, was hopping and fluttering about and chattering to himself.

"Yes, yes, yes. The end of your rope, I see. Though two heads are better than one, so to speak. You took the words right out of my mouth. It's plain as day, I'll make no bones about it. You don't have a moment to lose."

"Chester," Pteros Chronos spoke slowly. He had transformed into a strong direct flashlight beam shining right into the magpie's eyes. "Do you remember who it was who traded for the airplane?"

"Certainly," chirped Chester, obviously relieved to have the answer. "Bright as a new penny, I am, I am. It was the professor. That early bird. Traded with a full bag of whatnots. Wanted to use your airplane as a model. Got a suitcase, too. Nothing will come of it. Lots of hot air, that Professor! You can't believe a word of it. Head's in the clouds. Got a screw loose, too."

"And where might we find this professor?" asked Pteros Chronos.

"Beyond the Sheers...if you get my drift. Put a feather in your cap, and look both ways. Lives in a cave, in a jumble of big rocks. Yes, indeed, put your best foot forward when you go see the professor. A strange old bird, if you know what I mean." The magpie hopped closer to Anthony and said in a quieter voice, "You'll be good as new in no time flat. That's the ticket. Good as new!"

But it did take some time for Anthony to stop crying, and some more time for Chester to explain to Pteros Chronos how to find the Sheers. They unrolled Jim's map and in that space previously filled with sea serpents and labeled *Unknown Territory*, the magpie showed them where the mountainous Sheers sat behind three hills. On the far side of the Sheers was the tumble of rocks where the professor lived in a cave, though the magpie was quick to say he'd never been there himself.

"So I've been told. Never knew a soul to travel there. Even for birds...you know, birds of a feather...wind too strong. Take my word for it. All might go haywire if you don't know the ropes. That's it...in a nutshell."

CHAPTER 32

Endeavor, Steadfast, and Valor

From the leafy green trees of the Trading Post along the river they climbed into a hilly landscape, barren and strange. Here there were few trees, and those were blackish and thorny and offered no shade. Singular large boulders were scattered about, casting faint shadows on the hard ground. There was no path, and the rocks crouching here and there caused Anthony and Pteros Chronos to zigzag as they climbed. Twisting far below them on their right and guiding them was the Endless.

The wind had increased as they neared the crest of the first hill. They decided to stop and rest and it was from here that they finally saw the Sheers, an immense ridge of glassy peaks which stretched along the Endless and disappeared into the clouds.

"Magnificent!" whispered Pteros Chronos.

"Wow! Those are really big mountains! Do you think they are made of ice, Pteros Chronos?"

"It's difficult to determine from here. I'm led to believe they are crystal in nature. Certainly something quite translucent...hmm...Anthony, are you familiar with that word, *translucent*?"

"Yes, I do know that word. It's about letting light through. I think those mountains have a torch inside them. The rocks have turned the switch on...to let the light through."

"Well, there is certainly light coming from somewhere. Perhaps it is from within, though I've never thought of rocks as light bearers. There is a difference, Anthony, between being a bearer of light and being simply a reflector." Pteros Chronos had strong feelings about this. "Shall we try one of Mr. Watchit's muffins?" He expanded brightly, as a true bearer of light.

Anthony reached into the paper bag. He read the handwritten label. "*Endeavor*. What does that mean?"

Pteros Chronos nibbled on a tiny bite from the muffin Anthony held out to him, pausing while Anthony took a bite as well. Both of them chewed silently, tasting and swallowing with some effort.

"Endeavor means to try." He spoke in a voice quite crowded by dry muffin. Swallowing caused him to enlarge and shimmer. "But not just once," he continued, clearing his throat. "To try again and again, even when things get rough. Trying on and on. It's precisely what we are doing now in searching for your airplane, Anthony." He took another bite, though smaller. "It is a perfect word for our journey. Especially timely as we approach the Sheers. By the way, do you taste cauliflower...just the hint of cauliflower?"

Anthony was already struggling with his tiny bite of Endeavor. "Cauliflower! Who would make a muffin out of cauliflower?" A good bit of gagging followed. Anthony's eyes watered. His face turned red. "Do you think we could leave the rest here for the creatures who come in the night? My dad always says we should leave just a little food for the animals." Anthony tried smiling his hopeful smile.

"A splendid idea, Anthony. Quite generous, indeed. Though I must say that I believe these word muffins are mostly food for thought. They don't magically make us try harder or act braver or kinder, but they do put the word in our mouths, and the thoughts in our heads. They give us an idea to chew on, and that's no small thing for a muffin to do."

They sampled two other muffins, *Steadfast* and *Valor*.

Steadfast was green and broke apart with difficulty. When Pteros Chronos suggested spinach as a main ingredient, Anthony explained that he already knew the word *steadfast* from the fairy tale about the tin soldier with only one leg.

"Valor. Ahh...that's a word worth trying," said Pteros Chronos. "It reminds me of the tale of the brave mouse who frees the lion caught in the trap. That was a story of valor!"

"And friendship," said Anthony. "The mouse promised to help the lion no matter what. Just like you, Pteros Chronos. You're helping me find my airplane, no matter what."

Anthony took a small bite of Valor and scrunched up his face.

"Yuck. Yuck, yuck, yuck. I think this was made from acorns. I know this taste. I made an acorn stew once when I was camping with my dad. I have already tasted Valor. It's in my head."

"Well, indeed. I think we are well equipped for the rest of our journey. Mr. Watchit's muffins have encouraged us with thoughts of Endeavor, Steadfast, and Valor. I believe we are ready to meet the Sheers."

And with that, Anthony and Pteros Chronos left the hilltop. They felt energized and happy. They chatted and laughed, and Pteros Chronos sang a song he wrote called "Starry Nights," and then together they sang several verses of "Swing Low, Sweet Chariot," a song both had learned from their grandmothers.

The only signs of their passage were three tiny mounds of crumbs, and those disappeared before morning. An ancient tortoise and a traveling company of field mice shared the leftovers. They were later honored for exceptional bravery and determination.

CHAPTER 33

The Sheers

Anthony did not know the word *formidable*. When Pteros Chronos described the Sheers as formidable, Anthony thought he meant huge or beautiful, for they were light-filled and enormous crystal peaks.

Though Anthony knew about fear—scorpions and tetanus shots and the big black dog down the street and clowns when he was quite small and, most recently, crossing a wide river in a small boat during a bad storm—he had never been afraid of heights. So much climbing around on the Boulders had developed in him an affection and admiration for rocks of all sorts, especially big rocks. His windowsill at home held a collection of quartz crystals, the very mountainous material that stood before him now and would lead him to his airplane. When he looked up at the Sheers, Anthony found he was simply not afraid.

For Pteros Chronos, however, there was something unsettling about these mountains glistening with light on such a sunless afternoon. As he scouted about for a place to begin their climb, he quickly realized his light, even his strongest beam, disappeared against the radiance of these rocks. Such an experience was new to him, and, for a moment, he felt off-balance. For a moment he questioned his assignment as guide and bearer of light. But being a creature of great inner strength (he liked to use the word *fortitude*), this uneasiness lasted but a moment. He knew he must confront his limitations and move on. He did.

"Anthony, over here," he said, raising his voice against a wind that whipped about. "I believe this may be a route worth investigating." Anthony finished retying his shoelaces and joined Pteros Chronos where a steep, armlike part of the mountain joined the ground. Pteros Chronos was attempting to spotlight a narrow track which topped the ridge, though his beam was too faint. He quickly resumed his orb shape and flew closer to Anthony. "I find my light insufficient, Anthony. I cannot seem to outshine these strange rocks. An unexpected problem, though perhaps a temporary one and for me alone. The important thing is that you will have plenty of light to see the route, even though it will be other light."

"But you will be with me, Pteros Chronos. That's the most important thing."

"Well, yes. But come here. Do you see this beginning track?" He whirred up the steep ridge, and Anthony could see a flatness that topped the glassy slope. It was wide enough for a small climber, but, combined with this wind, not large enough for mistakes. "I must warn you, Anthony. There is nothing on either side of this track. Nothing to hold to, nothing to balance against, nothing to keep you from falling should you slip. The Endless is far, far below on this side..." and Pteros Chronos moved over into the air on the right side of the trail. "Those thorn trees are now a dense forest on the other side. You will need to be very careful, Anthony. Watch your every step."

"Don't worry, Pteros Chronos. I feel very brave. I am a good climber. I promise to pay attention. I think I should leave this sack of cookies from Mr. Watchit and Jim's map here. I don't want to have anything in my hands."

"A very good idea, Anthony. Though might I suggest that you put one cookie into your pocket, just in case the professor has not prepared dinner for us." They laughed together as Anthony gently arranged the map and the bag of cookies, minus one, at the base of the Sheers.

"I'll go ahead of you, Anthony. My light is of no use to you, but I have a strong voice. I shall be your scout, your lookout. I will advise you of trail conditions, step by step. Shall we proceed?"

Anthony pulled up his jacket hood, and they began. Pteros Chronos counted each step aloud. "...five...six ...seven..."

Anthony found the track narrower than he expected. It did not allow room for both feet together, so his climb was more like an aerial balancing act. There was no safe way to stop once he started, placing one foot in front of the other. He was right. He did need his hands free for balancing.

"Pteros Chronos! I am a tightrope walker!"

"...twenty-five...twenty-six...twenty-seven. Yes, you are doing wonderfully. Keep it up, Anthony... thirty...thirty-one...Pay attention."

They continued, up and up and up with Pteros Chronos counting each step and Anthony trying hard to concentrate.

"...fifty-six...fifty-seven...fifty-eight..."

But keeping up such close attention, even on a dangerous mountain trail, is difficult for a small boy. Even as Pteros Chronos continued his steady counting and even as Anthony's feet stayed on the track, his mind began to wander.

Anthony marveled at this trail. He wondered how this glassy ridge had become a flat track, maybe five or six inches wide, and he wished for a ruler. He wondered if some giant simply cut off the top of the ridge thousands of years ago and what sort of a saw could shave rock. That led him to remember Horace Rumpus and the view from his hand high above the OUATs. Had Horace ever traveled here? Did he know about the Sheers? And what was Mr. Watchit doing, and were the OUATs settling around campfires to listen to stories?

"...seventy-five...seventy-six...seventy-seven... keep going, Anthony. We are not far from the clouds now."

Anthony thought some more about Mr. Watchit and wondered if he would ever see him again. He remembered that he had not given him his address again, after it was lost when the traveling bag floated down the Endless. He thought about the wind and decided the last time he had felt wind like this was in the Nest of the Boulders, that very day the airplane had disappeared. He wondered if he had ever been this high before, and he glanced below at the Endless, now a thin grey line threading itself through a narrow chasm on his right.

It was exactly at that moment that he heard a muffled sound. It seemed to be above him. The clouds were so close now that when Anthony looked up, he felt a thick puff of cloud blow around him. At the same time Pteros Chronos (his counting now at step ninety-six) warned him of loose material on the track ahead.

It was all too much. When Anthony looked up, he lost his rhythm and more important, his balance and his footing. Instantly he felt himself slip off the track.

His small hands grabbed for the edge, his whole body smushed against the face of the crystal precipice, and his feet dangled in space. The wind was blowing, blowing, and all of this happened under the cover of cloud.

Pteros Chronos was immediately there beside Anthony's face, speaking in a firm voice.

"Hang on, Anthony. Hang on. Can you pull yourself up? Pull! Pull! I sense that help is coming. I will surround you with my light. Hang on. Steadfast, Anthony! Steadfast!"

Just at that critical moment when the rest of this story hung by the small arms of Anthony Bartholomew Mandopolis, several amazing things happened rather quickly.

That blowing sounded closer. Anthony could see nothing but the crystal wall, cold and scratching against his face, but he was certain there was something behind him. A something which hovered.

"What is it, Pteros Chronos? What's behind me?"

But Pteros Chronos's voice was not what he heard.

"A visitor? A visitor?" the voice said.

More movement behind him. Perhaps a sound of gears.

Pteros Chronos was whirring very near his right ear, and for a moment, Anthony decided that was the noise he had heard.

"Something's behind you, Anthony. A kind something, perhaps a kind someone, though I can't be sure.

It is hidden in cloud. Be brave, Anthony. We have few choices at the moment. But if you fall, I shall accompany you."

For this tiny bit of time, which seemed a long bit of time to Anthony, when he knew he could not hold on much longer and the blowing sounds increased, a bulky something brushed against his legs and then brushed again...all of this happening in less than five blinks of an eye.

Then, a clear command.

"Let go, Small Boy. Let go. Just drop."

And drop he did.

CHAPTER 34

Professor Wingett

Anthony fell hard, tearing his jacket, scratching his nose and elbows as he fell, and landing in a heap on the very edge of something. Something that swayed and tipped dangerously. He knew immediately he could fall again, for whatever he had fallen on was wildly off balance.

Clouds and swirling mist blinded him, and yet somehow a vision of Mr. Watchit standing up in Ratty's small boat appeared clearly in his mind. Was this a warning? Anthony bunched himself into the smallest possible ball, searched with his hands for direction, and realized he was indeed on a very narrow platform. He inched—slowly, slothlike—toward center.

The platform responded. The tipping stopped.

"Well done, Small Boy," spoke the voice from behind him. "Now, remain very still. I have not tested for the sudden impact of additional weight. Do not move. Give the cloudboard time to right itself." It was a strong voice, commanding yet not unkind, and it blew through the boiling clouds behind him.

Anthony peeked through the cracks between his arms to find Pteros Chronos signaling him through the fog.

"Dot, dot, dot...dot, dot, dot...dot, dot, dot."

"Pteros Chronos!" he whispered, greatly relieved to see his friend. "Where am I? What's a cloudboard?"

"I have no information at all," he whispered back, causing his already faint light to blur with the effort. "But we are in the clouds. You seem to be positioned on something boardlike—"

A clanking noise interrupted him, and Anthony felt the sensation of forward movement. "I believe the voice belongs to the same someone who now pilots this cloudboard craft," he whispered again, whirring so close that Anthony felt wings brush softly across his right ear.

Anthony lifted his head, feeling moisture on his face and finding he could see more than before. They were traveling gently upward through thick mountains of cloud, but not in a straight line. In fact, they seemed to be following a kind of twisting path between bulging puffy clouds, around hilly cloud mounds, through dark cloud tunnels, and occasionally very near the edges of clouds where sunlight shafted through and Anthony briefly glimpsed the narrow board beneath him.

Quite unexpectedly they popped up and into the sunlight. A blue sky stretched above them, and the clouds glistened and swirled below them like a spread of meringue.

He was sitting in the middle of a long board, maybe eight feet long and about three feet wide. Anthony noticed it tapered to an upturned point in front, reminding him of elf shoes. Turning around slowly and carefully, he saw someone wearing brown aviator goggles and a tight-fitting aviator cap and sitting several feet behind him at a small steering wheel. Until the pilot smiled and waved, Anthony thought perhaps Mr. Watchit had tricked them and was, in fact, this pilot and owner of the voice. But the smile changed that. It was not Mr. Watchit, even though those goggles looked much like his.

"Very fine transition," the pilot said. "We are at a cruising altitude now, simply afloat on these lovely thermals. Look! Would you just LOOK at this cloudscape! Have you ever seen anything so beautiful?"

"No." Anthony shook his head without turning back around. "I've never done this before either."

"Ever wanted to fly, Small Boy?"

"I've always wanted to fly," Anthony replied, still speaking over his shoulder and holding tightly to the edges of the cloudboard. "I even tried it once, from the top of the Boulders. I wanted to fly to Far Away, but I landed here instead."

"Hmmm, Far Away? I'm wondering where that might be. But, you are certainly flying now, Small Boy. The cloudboard allows us to experience flight almost like the birds, though without the effort. I will explain all of this later when we land. Shall we just enjoy the view for now?"

"Uh-hmm. Excuse me," Pteros Chronos whirred and blazed about. It was a dramatic effect. "I am wondering, Captain Pilot Person, when you plan to descend. You see, we are in a bit of a hurry."

"Oh my! My, my, my! I didn't know there were two of you! Or that one of you was Pure Brilliance. Goodness! My goggles must be foggy not to have seen YOU!"

Pteros Chronos burst into a series of firework displays, including red and blue lights which Anthony knew he saved for special occasions. He finished with a zippy fly-about which spangled the whole cloudboard in a shower of light crystals. Even Anthony was impressed.

"Wow! Bravo! Bravo! You ARE something to see," continued the pilot. "How did I miss you? And could it be that you have helicopter capacity?"

"Indeed. We Time Flies refer to in-place whirring as hovering. And to be precise, it is a very advanced skill among winged creatures. Helicopters, I believe, have been designed by imitation, scientifically speaking." Pteros Chronos paused here and cleared his throat, just for emphasis. "But, back to the question of time. When do you expect to land, kind pilot? We are on a schedule."

"Oh, yes, landing." The pilot paused, distracted perhaps by this brilliant orb that could speak politely and hover—at the same time. "I certainly understand keeping to a schedule. That's a cornerstone in scientific work. Though I always lean toward spontaneous invention and creativity in my particular field of science. I simply thought the small boy would enjoy an excursion after such a frightful adventure on the Sheers."

In the pause that followed Anthony tried to remember the details of his 'frightful adventure on the Sheers' when the pilot commanded loudly, "Prepare for landing!"

"Prepare for landing? How do we prepare?" Anthony's voice sounded small. "What do we do?"

"Nothing really, Small Boy," the pilot laughed. "I just love to say those words. They are so *aeronautical*. Just hold on tight. We may experience some *turbulence*. I love that word, too."

The cloudboard shuddered slightly as they descended and were swallowed again by the hungry, swarming clouds. Anthony knew airplanes flew with instruments in cloudy conditions, and he wondered what instruments this pilot used now. He had seen nothing but the steering wheel.

However, in no time at all they were floating gently downward. When Anthony looked at the clouds now above him, he saw that a large blue umbrella had opened, softening their descent. Below them a green meadow swayed. It was park like with tall trees here and there around the edges and a large heap of boulders in the middle. Except for the Sheers, which Anthony saw towering along the far side of the park, it all looked very familiar.

Coughing and sputtering, the cloudboard shook a bit as they glided low to the ground and landed in a series of bumps. Anthony stood up, relieved to feel ground under his feet.

The pilot, wearing heavy, brown combat boots and a camouflage jumpsuit, stepped gracefully off the cloudboard and extended a right hand toward Anthony.

"Welcome, Small Boy and Brilliant Light," said the pilot, removing the goggles and the aviator cap to reveal an explosion of curly red hair, dangly turquoise earrings, large brown eyes, and a soft, smiling face.

"Oh! You're a lady!" said Anthony, wondering how he could have ever thought this pilot was a disguised Mr. Watchit.

"Indeed, Anthony, a lady and a pilot and..." Pteros Chronos was about to say 'a beauty,' but he was interrupted.

"Yes. I am Professor Wingett. Amelia Wright Wingett."

"You're the Professor?" Anthony looked quickly at Pteros Chronos to make sure he heard.

"Yes, I am Professor Wingett. Professor of *Ornithology*, retired. Ornithology is the study of birds, as I am certain you know, Brilliant Light," she nodded and smiled at Pteros Chronos. "I changed my name when I was about your age," she said, turning to Anthony. "Fascinated all my life with flying. So when I turned twelve, I stopped calling myself Judysue. I asked my parents and my friends to call me Amelia. It worked. And what about you two? How are you called?"

"I am Anthony. Anthony Bartholomew Mandopolis. I am just nine years old, not twelve. And this is my friend Pteros Chronos, spelled with a silent *P*. He's a Time Fly. He's helping me find my airplane."

Pteros Chronos, now the size of a cantaloupe whirred and glowed.

"Anthony, Anthony, hmmmm." Professor Wingett looked hard at Anthony. "Your name is familiar to me."

"Well, Madame Professor," began Pteros Chronos. "When we met Chester, the Magpie at the . . ."

". . . at the Trading Post," Professor Wingett burst in. "Of course! You're the Anthony of the Airplane! So, you're the creator of that amazing craft. A marvel of aerodynamic genius. Such lift. Such delicate curve in the wings. I knew I had to study that airplane, though I must admit that I read the note inside. Invasion of privacy to be sure. But unintentional. I thought it might contain some information I needed."

"Well, that's the note," explained Anthony, "from my teacher. My parents need to sign it, and I have to take it back to school. I'm being responsible."

Anthony paused with those words—such ordinary, everyday words, so unlike anything he had lately experienced and yet so comforting. And in explaining the reason for the note—his problem with daydreaming, with using his time—it was as if the place where he stood, with Pteros Chronos softly beaming good will and Professor Wingett listening eagerly, became peopled with his parents, the carolers in the snow globe, Mr. Trippett wearing the golden kite necktie, and all his friends in Mrs. Quickett's third grade classroom, and all of them were listening to his story.

"Well, as for time," Professor Wingett's gentle voice interrupted his imaginings. "I know I am simply ahead of my time. I'm a dreamer, too. How would the world work without dreamers like us, Anthony? We dreamers operate on a different time, don't we, Anthony." And she smiled a big happy smile at him. "This cloudboard you have just sailed upon," and she pointed with her combat boot. "That was simply a dream in the beginning. Like a puff of cloud, nothing more. But I figured and planned and experimented and made mistakes and worked some more and..."

"Did you crash?" Anthony squinted his eyes, remembering his fall from the Sheers and considering the danger in the life of the test pilot standing before him.

"Several times, though I see you, too, have the marks of a close encounter with the Sheers. A small price to pay for seeing a dream become something real."

"Something actual." Anthony nodded and looked toward Pteros Chronos, who was whirring around the cloudboard.

"Let me show you my dream," said the Professor. "You see, it is both glider and self-propelled craft, using water vapor from the clouds as a clean energy source." She pointed to a small black box at the far end of the board. "Here is the converter box. A simple transaction goes on inside. Water vapor from clouds enters through this opening. Friction from the foot pedals creates energy, which changes vapor to steam." She pointed to the pedals. "Steam powers the cloudboard when the lovely thermals are not around to keep us afloat…for then, Anthony, we are so much like a boat, adrift in the sea of the sky."

She ended her explanation with a dreamy gaze, which settled on the blue umbrella with multicolored peace signs. "Landing gear," she said, pointing to the umbrella. "Simplicity in design. And offering no resistance when not in use. I like the message too. Peace. Above all, peace.

"I am still dreaming about how to use this cloud-board. On some days I see it as pure sport. Just me and the board and the heavens. Such harmony. Such grace and joy!"

"Such races!" grinned Anthony, his eyes wide with the thought. "If you just had two cloudboards, we could race now, all through the clouds."

"Well, yes, races perhaps. But on other days I simply want to be of service, you know, using the cloud-board as a delivery vehicle. And now that I have that suitcase..." Professor Wingett looked up into the sky, envisioning something Anthony could not quite see.

"You have a suitcase?" he asked.

"Yes, it is quite a well-traveled bag, but it fits perfectly onto the back of the cloudboard. I have not yet tried it on a flight. Filled, it might be too heavy. There are still questions to be answered should I move in this direction. The biggest question is how would I find time to continue with my experiments, if I began a business? Choices, Anthony. Life is about making choices. How are we to spend our time?"

"Well, speaking of time, Professor Wingett, we are somewhat short on it right now." Pteros Chronos bobbed about in what Anthony knew indicated impatience. "Do you have Anthony's airplane? If so, may we have it, please?"

"Certainly you may have it." Professor Wingett smiled again and patted Anthony gently on the back.

"I do get off track. One thing leads to another and, before you know it, I'm..."

"You're Far Away," laughed Anthony. "Just like me."

"Yes, Far Away." She paused and took such a big breath she seemed to grow taller by a few inches. "Well," she smiled, "you two just follow me up the path." She turned abruptly and began walking toward the pile of large rocks she had earlier called the Tumbles. "Watch your step. Pay attention. Lots of *debris* left over from my experiments." Professor Wingett spoke over her shoulder. "You know, 'Creative Minds are Rarely Tidy!' That's what my mother used to tell me."

She led them at a brisk pace, and very soon they reached a well-worn path that wound itself up and through large boulders. More and more Anthony sensed he had walked this way before.

CHAPTER 35

Return Flight

The game began because he was so far behind and so weary.

Bone-tired weary, Anthony thought to himself, remembering how his grandmother used to say those words when she'd pull off her thick-heeled black shoes and settle into the old red rocking chair on their front porch. He could almost hear it creaking as she rocked, back and forth, back and forth.

"I'm bone-tired weary," he said quietly to himself. Just hearing those familiar words of hers was comfort. "I'm bone-tired weary!" he said again and louder, though neither the professor nor Pteros Chronos heard him.

They were too far ahead on a steep, zigzaggy trail to what Professor Wingett called the Perch. It was both her home and her lab. She and Pteros Chronos chatted as they climbed.

Anthony could not hear their conversation because he was so far behind and because the large rocks blocked their words. He only caught bits and pieces. That's when the game began.

" ... barometric pressure ... certainly ... lift ... doubtful ... helicopter ... horizontal ... balance ... secret ... "

Single words slipped down to him, and he began to wonder if words slid down easier than they climbed up. As far as he could tell neither Professor Wingett nor Pteros Chronos had heard any of his words from below. Maybe it was because it was harder for words to move up. Maybe it was because the boulders were in the way. Gradually he began imagining the boulders as giant Word Snatchers. They were guards, blocking the passage of phrases, even whole sentences, though some words slipped by. They were too fast or too slippery to catch. They were the Passwords.

Anthony stopped and listened. More Passwords.

" ... remarkable ... finally ... ornithologist ... hummingbird ... "

These Passwords scooted around the corners of the stony guards. They slipped over their bulky frames and tiptoed through small rocky crevices around their stone ankles. They arrived near enough that Anthony heard them—and what he heard was a call for help. They needed Anthony. For their word companions were left behind, within the prisons formed by the rock giants. There was no time to spare in this rescue.

Just as Anthony was devising a plan to save the captured words (before their terrible tortures began), Pteros Chronos called to him from above. Somehow all of his words found a straight flight right to Anthony. They arrived breathless and a little impatient.

"Can you hurry along, Anthony? We're up here."

Anthony looked up.

"I'm bone-tired weary," he said again, this time certain his words flew through the tight boundaries of the rock giants. "My tennis shoes have rubbed a blister on my toe, and my nose hurts." Anthony's words had a limping sound, and there was some stumbling among the phrases that followed. "And my jacket...I think my jacket is torn...and...I don't know what to do...after I get my airplane...What do I do next?...when it's time to go home...Pteros Chronos?"

"Next?" Pteros Chronos quickly whirred down to speak quietly right next to Anthony. There was no problem with the words getting through now. Pteros Chronos was close. His words were clear and direct. "Let's do one thing at a time. First we need to find your plane. I believe it is within Professor Wingett's laboratory, which is quite close. It's right up there. Just a few more small steps, Anthony."

"But after I find the airplane, how will I get home again? I don't know the way back. Will you come with me, Pteros Chronos?"

"I will be with you as long as you need me, Anthony. I promised that. And, in a manner of speaking, I will never be far away. Even when you are home, I will be near. You may not always see me, but this is also a promise. I will always be near."

"Always?"

"Always."

And so Anthony followed Pteros Chronos up the last bit of trail leading them to the tiptop of the Tumbles. There they found Professor Wingett smiling and waiting.

"Welcome," she said, her eyes bright with excitement. "I think you may be my first guests. I've tried to keep my whereabouts secret, but it proved to be unnecessary. The Sheers alone have been like a drawbridge to a castle. No one climbs the Sheers. The birds don't even fly this way. Too much wind. That's a pity. I would enjoy their company from time to time.

"So here is what I call The Perch," she continued, stretching her arms out wide to include the whole space where they stood, seeming to Anthony to be so close to the sky and, again, very familiar. "This is my launching pad. The cloudboard responds well at this elevation. It's just high enough, without the dangerous height of the Sheers. The wind here can become strong and quite often the clouds..." Professor Wingett talked on and on about lift and air pressure, gesturing excitedly, her arms flapping like wings.

Anthony tried to pay attention, but instead of making sense of her words, spoken so close to him, he thought about how they arrived without struggle. He had successfully passed all the Word Snatchers on the trail below. Now he and Pteros Chronos and Professor Wingett could send their words to one another without worry of their capture. Anthony was so distracted by the word game that he missed most of the phrases and sentences sent his way.

"...so, just watch your head, Anthony. It's a little tight getting inside, but then there is plenty of room."

Anthony followed her and her words through the rocky crack. Pteros Chronos whirred and glowed behind him.

Perhaps it was Anthony's distraction with the word game. Perhaps it was his weariness or that he was simply overwhelmed by what he saw when he entered the cave. Whatever the reason, he would never be able to describe Professor Wingett's lab with much accuracy.

Forever, in all the retellings of his adventure, this place would remain a cloudy blur to him. He would remember a huge chamber, lit by lots of lights that hung on heavy cords from the ceiling, though he would not remember seeing the ceiling. He would recall strange bookcases, also suspended from the ceiling and double sided so that, at the slightest touch, the cases would turn, revealing hundreds of books on the other side. He would remember the Professor showing him how to "flip" the bookcases. *Flip* was the very word she had used. He would remember that clearly.

He would remember following her into a corner of the cave, past a small daybed with a quilt much like the one his grandmother Ellis had made for him. In this corner, again hanging from an invisible ceiling, were hundreds, maybe thousands of model airplanes. Big charts lined the wall, one showing different wing designs of birds, and there was a long wooden table somewhere with what looked like the makings of a second cloudboard.

He would also remember how Professor Wingett climbed on a footstool and reached up to open a cabinet, and how it was locked, and how she had to climb back down and dig around in her backpack to find a single key, which was quite large, and Anthony would remember thinking it was too large to fit into the cabinet lock.

But it did fit. She opened the cabinet door, and there was the airplane! Finally!

"Watch, Pteros Chronos," she said, still standing on the top step of the footstool. "Watch the beauty of this flight. Grace in motion, that's what you're about to see. Are you ready, Anthony? I'm sending your airplane back to you. Get ready to catch it, Anthony."

She straightened her left arm, pointing toward Anthony. With her right arm back and her fingers gently holding the belly of the craft, she fixed her eyes on that invisible space above and beyond where the plane would sail upward and on and...

Shooooosh. She threw the airplane. Pteros Chronos whirred brightly as the plane angled toward Anthony and then, caught and held aloft by some sudden draft of wind, soared too high, beyond his reach and through the narrow cave opening and out into the late afternoon, and still it soared, with Anthony now running behind it, yelling "Stop! Wait, wait!" But the airplane felt the lovely lift of the thermals and circled in the freedom of fancy loops and swirls, and just at the moment when it swooped down a third time, Anthony, standing now on the tiptop rock, reached far enough and caught it.

"I got it! I got it! Pteros Chronos, Professor Wingett, I got my airplane! I finally got my airplane!"

And then, a stillness. A strange hush surrounded him, holding him gently. He sat in that stillness, clutching his airplane and waiting for Pteros Chronos and Professor Wingett and wondering where they were. His nose hurt from that fall against the Sheers. And he sat, waiting, waiting. It was so quiet, so still, Anthony felt sealed off, apart, as if time too had simply stopped.

Until a voice interrupted the quiet, "Anthony? Anthony? That you, buddy?"

Anthony looked around. A familiar voice. Was that Mr. Watchit calling him from below?

"Hey, Anthony. Are you up there, buddy? I'm coming up." In no time at all, Anthony's father's face was close to his. All his words came straight to Anthony. He heard all of them.

"We thought you might be up here, buddy. Mom saw Mr. Trippett at the hardware store. He was buying a kite. Told her you'd taken off for the park." His father's blue eyes misted just a bit, and he paused to catch his breath. "We were worried when you didn't come home after a while. You okay, buddy?"

"I'm great, Dad. I finally found my airplane," and he held the crumpled paper airplane out to him. "See, I found it. I finally found it."

His father took the airplane and, holding it gently, turned it around and around, inspecting it from all angles.

"Well, it looks to me like it's had quite a trip. You, too, Anthony buddy. Did you run into a wall with your nose?"

"Yes, sir. Something like that." Anthony took the airplane from his father, smoothed out its crumpled nose, and looked all around him. The wind had stopped, and he was sitting in the Nest of the Boulders.

With his father. And his airplane. "Can we go home now? I'm really hungry."

By the time they reached their front porch, the sun had dipped behind the trees, and the moon was rising. The evening sky was just beginning to wink with early stars.

"Look, Anthony. Polaris, right up there. See it?"

Anthony looked up to see the bright star.

It was blinking, "Dot, dot, dot."

Postscript

In the way of stories, we never really know the whole story, never the complete story, even if it is our own story. There are so many places to stand and listen and watch and wonder, so many ways to examine and puzzle over the events, the behaviors of characters, the slant of moonlight, the shape of rocks. We are given glimpses only, and the truth of those glimpses depends on where we are standing and how well we pay attention.

You and I, as readers, know almost as much as Anthony knows about this amazing adventure. We were standing in a good spot. We paid attention. But those who heard his story in the weeks and months afterward caught only bits and pieces. He never told anyone, even his parents, the whole of it. He left out episodes that would be upsetting to them like the crossing of the Endless in Ratty's tiny boat and being lifted high above a valley by Horace Rumpus. He told Mr. Trippett about Mr. Watchit and the Wordery, and one day during library, after Miss Bookit had finished reading *The Tale of Despereaux*, he burst out with "Carry the Torch! Listen for the Story!" The laughter that followed was enough to squelch any telling of his time with the OUATs or of Professor Wingett's cloudboard.

For Anthony, as you know, was not a bragger. He quickly realized that sharing these adventures would mean introducing Pteros Chronos, Mr. Watchit, Ratty, and all of his new friends to a world of many eager doubters. Somehow that seemed careless, even unkind. He knew there were things too magical to be explained. And so Anthony kept mostly quiet about his adventure.

Though on the day of his return, his story continued in ways mysterious. These events are additions and so fit into something called a *postscript*. If you have ever written a letter and, after signing it, remembered something you needed to include and so added a PS, you know about a postscript. It is word #47 in Anthony's dictionary. We could also call it an After Adventure. Are you paying attention?

Shortly after Anthony got home, hugged his mother, washed his face and hands, and ate a huge plate of spaghetti with tiny meatballs and lots of garlic breadsticks, he began to explain where he had been and what had happened. There were few details in this telling for he was, as you remember, "bone-tired weary," but he did explain that the rip in his jacket came from falling off a glass mountain, whereupon his mother looked directly at his father with large questioning eyes. And when Anthony took off his jeans and a scattering of cookie crumbs fell on the bathroom floor, he explained that Mr. Watchit had given them cookies from the Wordery.

Anthony picked up the label, which had also fallen on the floor, and said, "This cookie was *Persevere.* I know that means to keep at something until you finish it because Pteros Chronos told me it was a close cousin to Steadfast. We ate Steadfast before we crossed the Sheers. Steadfast was a muffin." He yawned.

At this point in the evening the whole bone-tired weary Mandopolis family went to bed. A new day was fast approaching and, though the porch light would not turn off that night, they all slept soundly.

The next day Anthony went to school, carrying the airplane note, signed by his parents. It was unusual to bring a paper airplane to a teacher, but Mrs. Quickett, after seeing that it had been properly signed, asked if Anthony wanted to keep it as a reminder. He had hoped she would ask this, and he promised to store it in his backpack during the day and that he would try hard to finish his work at school. His airplane, a reminder.

When he arrived home that afternoon, his mother handed him a many-folded piece of blue paper.

"It went right through the washer and the dryer, Anthony. I'm sorry. I found it in your back pocket when I folded your jeans."

Anthony took the folded note, now remembering that Ratty had handed him this poem on the bank of the Endless, remembering how he had been preoccupied with finding the OUATs and how he had forgotten about this gift.

"It's Ratty's poem," he said quietly, opening the folds to reveal a blank page. "It's gone. It's all washed away." His eyes filled with tears.

"Wait, Anthony. Look here, at the bottom." His mother pointed to a faint but very fancy capital R still visible in the bottom right corner.

"That's Ratty's R. For his name." Anthony was sniffling now, "soft crying," his mother called it. And being the sort of mother who knows the language of tears, she reasoned these tears fell from weariness.

"He was my friend, Mom. He took me across the Endless in his little boat. He wrote this poem for me, but I never read it. I was too busy. I forgot about it." His small shoulders now jerked with sobs. His mother handed him a used tissue from her apron pocket, noting the possibility of real sorrow in her small son.

"Well, Anthony," his mother said in that soothing tone reserved for mothers. "We all get busy and forget to do some things we meant to do. Tell me about Ratty, Anthony. Was he a little boy your age?"

"No, Mom. He was a rat." He paused here to blow his nose and wipe away tears with the back of his hand. "THE Rat in *The Wind in the Willows*, Mom. I met him. He fixed us stew, wonderful stew, and he has a garden with radishes. We camped out in his backyard."

Later that afternoon when his father came home from work, Anthony walked with him to the Boulders. He wanted to show his father the portal, that crack between the rocks where he first entered the large cave and met Pteros Chronos. But, though they hiked up and down and crisscrossed that mound of boulders, they found nothing. Nothing. The Boulders were solid, sealed tight and silent. At one point Anthony thought he heard distant whirring, but they never found any clue that the Boulders provided an entrance for Anthony's airplane or the adventure he had described.

However, the following week, a story ran in the local paper about scientists who had reported recent *seismic tremors* in a wide area that included Centerville. A spokesperson said, "Significant internal shifting was possibly due to a series of earthquakes too small to be detected by residents, but large enough to cause changes within the earth." 'Rearranging' was one of the words used by a geologist with the National Earthquake Information Center.

"Hmm..." said Anthony's father when he read the article the next morning at breakfast. He showed it to Anthony's mother.

"Hmm..." she said.

Then there were the light incidents. Many light incidents. It seemed that wherever Anthony went, amazing and unexplained light went along, too. His bicycle light always beamed "dot, dot, dot," even if he had not turned it on. At scout campouts, the campfire blazed all night, even when there was no wood left burning. When Anthony attended birthday parties, the candles could not be blown out, even if the mother insisted she had positively NOT bought those trick candles. Warm glows inside his closet or under his bed often woke him in the night, and the Fourth of July fireworks display from Anthony's backyard was so spectacular that all of Centerville heard about it. And that porch light, which would not turn off the first night he returned, continues to beam light to this day.

It was around Halloween when the most amazing after-adventure happened. Anthony had come home from school to find his mother waiting for him on the front porch.

There was hurry in her eyes.

"Did you have a good day?" She smiled quickly at him, and not waiting for his answer, asked, "Do you know anything about a brown bag, Anthony?"

"What kind of bag, Mom?" He squinted and stopped halfway up the porch steps. Given all the after-adventures, none of which passed him unnoticed, he was alert to any strange happening. You see, he had learned to pay attention.

"Well, it's an old brown leather bag. I found it right in the middle of the front yard, just an hour ago. It wasn't here this morning, I'm sure of that. I was right here this morning, setting out chrysanthemums, and it wasn't here. It has your name on it, Anthony. I haven't opened it. Do you know anything about it, sweetie? Do you think it's just a Halloween prank of some kind?"

There was hurry in her words, too. Mrs. Mandopolis had grown somewhat accustomed to the unexplained events occurring since that day back in March, but, still, she was Anthony's mom, after all. We cannot hold it against her that she viewed her job as protector a little more seriously.

While she had explained all this, Anthony had joined her on the porch.

"Where, Mom? Where's the bag?"

"I set it over there, behind the ficus tree. Be careful, Anthony. We don't know what's inside."

Anthony walked around the corner of their porch.

There it was. Mr. Watchit's traveling bag, sitting under the ficus tree like a Christmas present. A tag tied around the handles read, *Anthony*.

"Oh!" Anthony gasped. "Oh, Mom, do you know what this is? This is Mr. Watchit's bag, his traveling bag. It's the very one. I KNOW this bag, Mom."

Anthony's mother had followed him around the corner. She sat down next to him on the porch floor.

"I know this bag," he repeated, turning it over, inspecting it, feeling it, remembering. "It carried everything we needed...a little blue teapot and a funny burner Mr. Watchit made himself, and all sorts of things to eat, even egg-salad sandwiches, and aviator goggles...but I think Professor Wingett has those goggles now. I wonder where all that stuff is now?"

His mother sat quietly, offering no explanation, knowing she had no explanation.

Anthony found the tarnished zipper pull and guided it around its toothy track. Even that slight sound, something he had heard again and again, was a memory. He pulled the bag wide enough to see inside, and the smell of old leather and tea bags and apricot scones and even Mr. Watchit filled the air around them, though only Anthony seemed to notice.

It was empty. Empty. It had once been so filled. Anthony closed his eyes to better imagine the blue teapot, the handmade burner, all those packets of food, the collapsible walking stick. Gently his hand moved inside, feeling the soft lining, moving around the corners, the bottom, the sides, something he had never done before. A slight bulge caught his attention, and he realized he had touched a concealed side pocket. It was a small pocket, stitched into the lining and zipped closed with a tiny zipper. Something round hid inside. Round and hidden. He looked inside just to make sure his hand was honest. Then he looked at his mother.

"Something IS inside, Mom. Inside this little pocket. I can feel it. See?" Anthony angled the open traveling bag toward his mother.

"Yes, I do see the pocket, Anthony. Well," she paused and smiled at him. "Don't you want to open it? The bag has your name on it."

Anthony worked the tiny zipped pocket open and carefully extended two fingers, scrunching up his eyes to imagine what he touched.

"It's round. I think it's a watch," said Anthony, looking upward and working to extract the round something. "I think maybe a pocket watch. I can feel a chain. Mr. Watchit had lots of pocket watches, Mom. Maybe this is the one he brought on our trip. Maybe he forgot he had packed it. Maybe..." Anthony stopped as his fingers fished out of the traveling bag a golden watch attached to a golden chain.

"Wow! Look at this, Mom. This is Mr. Watchit's for sure. He had so many pocket watches. This one must have been special."

Anthony turned the golden watch around and around, inspecting all the tiny flourishes and swirls that were engraved on the case. He pressed the tiny button that clicked open the cover, revealing a crystal watchface and hands that appeared to have stopped at two fifteen. He held the watch to his ear, listening for that pulse that told him the minutes were ticking away. There was no sound.

"Hmmm," mused his mother. "Two-fifteen? That's just about the time I found this bag, just an hour ago. Hmmm...well, it's very special, this bag and this watch, Anthony. Still..." Anthony's mother looked back out across the front yard, as if the answer to this strange mystery might be out there, in broad daylight.

"I'll keep this bag and the watch safe for Mr. Watchit. Right under my bed. Just in case he needs them. I'll know just where they are." Anthony paused. "And I'll keep Ratty's poem, well, the note with the fancy R, inside, too. For safekeeping." He added quietly, "That's just what I'll do."

His eyes shifted from his mother to a distant place, beyond their yard, beyond the clouds even. He had stopped crying.

Anthony and his mother sat very still for a long while, he just holding the brown bag in his lap and Mr. Watchit's pocket watch in his hand, and his mother just being there with him. Finally, he replaced the watch in its little pocket and zipped it closed. Then he zipped the traveling bag and sat it upright, its handles standing straight up, just like he last saw them. He ran his small hands over the skin of the bag, imagining, remembering those short sails atop a brown ship, floating down the Endless.

An Appendix of
Anthony's Math Story Problems

An appendix is a collection of extra material usually at the end of the book. It is something additional, and it is usually something "hanging" onto something larger. These story problems of Anthony's are attached to his larger story. Perhaps you have an appendix which is still attached to the larger YOU.

Problem #7: The Story of 37 + 6
One day the Centerville Zoo discovered that a careless zookeeper had left a door open and that their collection of 37 Gila monster lizards had slithered through the door and escaped from the zoo. They were roaming around town, riding the bus, swinging in the park, and scaring the citizens. The chief zookeeper knew that

Gila monsters could be tricky creatures, and so he sent out a posse of 37 junior zookeepers to find them and return them to the zoo. Then, on second thought, remembering that Gila monsters could be dangerous, he added 6 more junior zookeepers to help. How many zookeepers were sent? Do you think they found and returned every single Gila monster?

Problem #8: The Story of 37 – 6
An evil wizard sat on a dark throne in a dark dungeon, day after day. He never left, even to eat or sleep, for he was guardian of the 37 jewels of the kingdom. Those jewels were kept in a green wooden vase placed on a red table right in front of the wizard's throne. However, in the night, small mice had quietly gnawed a hole in the table and the vase and were stealing the jewels for their own kingdom within the castle walls. They loved the jewels for the light they reflected and they had stolen 6 jewels. How many jewels are left in the green vase? When do you think the wizard will notice the loss?

Problem #9: The Story of 37 × 6
Mrs. Quickett is a teacher and a saleslady. She works after school at a store called Time For All where she sells minutes. She has only worked there three months so she is not allowed to sell hours. Selling hours takes experience, and she will not have that for another two months.

Every minute costs 6 cents ($.06). A small boy needs to buy 37 minutes. Could you tell him how much money he will need? There is no tax. Minutes are not taxed.

Problem #10: The Story of 37 ÷ 6

A small boy lived with his parents and grandparents (on his father's side) and his 13 brothers in the Andes Mountains. He did not go to the village school, but he worked all day as a shepherd, herding a flock of 37 goats. At night he needed to drive the goats into 6 pens, which were crude but sturdy protection against mountain gorillas. But each pen could hold only 6 goats. How many goats were left alone, prey to the lurking gorillas? What should the little boy do?

Anthony's Dictionary

As you have probably noticed in reading Anthony's story, there are some words that are italicized. Most of these words come directly from Anthony's red spiral Dictionary where he collected them.

Here his words are listed in alphabetical order so they are easier to find. Often you will know the meaning (or close enough) from the way a word is used in the sentence. This is called the context. But, if you want to make sure, just use this list as a tool. The definition given fits the word's purpose in this context, though many words have many different meanings. You can find all the definitions in a complete dictionary.

Anthony would recommend that you begin your own collection too.

1. **acronym**: a word formed by initial letters of other words. OUATs stand for the Once Upon A Times.

2. **actual:** real

3. **aeronautical:** the science of making and flying aircraft

4. **appropriate**: suitable; fitting

5. **battlements:** in castles, a low wall built on towers and having up and down sections used as protection while defending the castle

6. **boisterous:** rough and noisy

7. **chronology:** things in the order in which they happened

8. **constellation**: a group of stars given a specific name

9. **cleft:** space or opening made by a split

10. **debris:** the remains of things broken or destroyed

11. **deluge**: great overflowing of water, as in a flood

12. **dungeon:** a strong underground cell usually for holding prisoners

13. **encoding:** to put a message into code

14. **endeavor:** to make every effort, to try

15. **erratics:** boulders transported from an original site to an unusual location

16. **formidable**: something of alarming size and strength

17. **fortitude:** moral strength, endurance

18. **illusion:** a misleading appearance or image

19. **immemorial:** going back in time beyond memory

20. **labyrinth:** a maze

21. **larder**: a pantry; a place to store food

22. **metronome:** a mechanical instrument for marking time in music

23. **mosaic:** a picture made with small pieces of stone or tile

24. **observant:** quick to notice; alert

25. **optimism:** a habit of looking on the bright side of things

26. **ornithology**: the study of birds

27. **persevere:** to keep trying despite difficulty

28. **port:** the left side of a ship or boat when you are facing the front (bow)

29. **portal:** a door; entrance

30. **portcullis:** a grate like fortification of iron or timber that guards the entrance to a castle

31. **postscript:** an addition to a letter after the letter has been signed, written as 'PS'

32. **preoccupied:** completely absorbed in thought

33. **preservationist:** someone who tries to preserve or save something

34. **pretense**: pretending to be something else; make-believe

35. **pseudonym:** a false name used by an author to hide his/her identity

36. **rendezvous**: a planned meeting

37. **responsible:** being trustworthy; accountable

38. **ruffian:** a tough, lawless person

39. **seismic tremors**: the shaking of the earth due to earthquakes

40. **sidetrack:** a trail or path off the main course of travel

41. **starboard:** the right side of a ship or boat when you are facing the front

42. **steadfast:** firm in purpose; determined

43. **surge:** a rush or sudden wave of water

44. **survey:** to look at carefully; to inspect

45. **surveillance**: the act of watching

46. **translucent:** letting light shine through

47. **troubadour:** a traveling singer of love songs

48. **tsunami:** seismic sea waves usually caused by earthquakes under or near the ocean

49. **turbulence:** disturbance; disorder

50. **turret:** a small tower attached to a larger structure, as in a castle

51. **unintentionally:** not meaning to; accidentally

52. **valor:** bravery; courage

Acknowledgments With Gratitude

Though my name sits on the cover of this book, I am just part of the authorship. That particular ship, much like Ratty's rowboat, crossed from one side of the river to the other with some very real and very mystical help. At times I guided the voyage. And, at other times, I was simply passenger. I believe that to be the nature of creativity.

I am deeply grateful for all the passengers who have traveled with me on Anthony's adventure. My family—generations, before and after, of readers, writers, teachers, philosophers, naturalists, dreamers, artists, runners, dancers and surfers. Thank you for providing me with safe harbors, stretching horizons, and life jackets. Friends—nudging me, questioning me, teaching me, inspiring me, affirming me. Thank you for your willingness to row the boat, to tend the sails, to power the engines. All the Anthonys I have met along the way and one, in particular, who is currently writing his own story. Thank you for carrying the Torch. Teachers and librarians who find time to nurture the imagination and creativity in children. Thank you, one and all!

—Susan Syers Stark

About The Author

Susan Syers Stark lives in the Texas Hill Country with her husband, three cats, a garden full of butterflies and visiting possums, raccoons and turkeys. She has spent much of her life in the company of children, sharing stories, spiders, birds and rocks. This is her first book. Learn more about Susan by visiting her at SusanSyersStark.com.

CPSIA information can be obtained at www.ICGtesting.com
Printed in the USA
LVOW07s1927290116

472145LV00002BB/6/P